The Carpetbaggers of Mbantua

Shan

February 2023

Edited by Jonathan Smith

Images on cover: Luxstorm/Pix

GW00499779

ISBN Ebook: 978-0-6457074-1-0

ISBN Print: 978-0-6457074-0-3

Clear Mind Press, Australia

Copyright © Shan

Legal deposit in the National Library of Australia

Design and layout: Clear Mind Press

Clear Mind Press: www.clearmindpress.com

Typesetting: Clear Mind Press - Baskerville 12

Cover Design: Clear Mind Press

The Carpetbaggers of Mbantua

Shan

We acknowledging all Aboriginal people, the Traditional Custodians of this land on which we gather today, and pay our respects to their Elders past and present. We extend that respect to Aboriginal and Torres Strait Islander peoples here today.

In Central Australia Indigenous people generally refer to themselves in English as 'Aboriginal', This book follows their example. The reference is used by local Aboriginal people and does not include Torres Strait Islanders.

The opinions expressed by the characters in this book are not the opinions of the author or the publisher.

About the book

In Alice Springs one can reinvent oneself. This is exactly what Hank Jefferson needs. His wife, Bettina, does not agree. Hank settles in Alice Springs nevertheless, and learns about the local art trade from Blue, a local Aboriginal man. Bettina's revenge does not work out the way she intended it to...

The dark world of the art trade in Alice Springs is described in this novella. Although they are located a short distance from town now, the painting sheds still exist to this day. Carpetbaggers are still roaming at dawn.

About the author

Shan is a promising upcoming Australian writer.
The Carpetbaggers of Mbantua is Shan's first published book.
Shan is now working on an epic novel that is written as a memoir, titled *Women!*
In the tradition of the European rock star of the memoir, Karl Ove Knausgård, the publication will contain several books.

Book one: *Crying Mothers*
Book two: *The Spirit of the Fox*
Book three: *Journey to the Edge of the Earth*

Keep up with Shan's work at:
www.clearmindpress.com

car ·pet ·bag ·ger; noun /kɑːpɪtbagə(r)/: outsider; especially: a non-resident or new resident who seeks private gain from an area, often by meddling in its business or politics.

In Alice Springs, one can reinvent oneself. Surrounded by deserts, it has developed its own laws of living. Everyone who his not Aboriginal is a stranger on this land that is also called Mbantua and that was once populated only by Aboriginal people who belonged to the Yiperinya, the Caterpillar Dreaming.

They simply call it: 'country'. They once moved from water hole to water hole, naked and in small groups. The men hunted for roo and iguana with spears and boomerangs, the women gathered bush tucker in crude wooden bowls, the children drew in the red sand with their fingers.

The groups spoke many different languages. They simply call them 'language'.

They did not build dwellings but sought shelter in caves or under trees and shrubs.

There were spirits everywhere, spirits to be feared and spirits to be loved, naughty spirits, happy spirits, and scary ones. They were in the rocks and the shrubs, in the waterholes and the clouds. The roaming spirits lived with the souls of the ancestors in the Dreamtime, and they ruled life and lore.

Thus, the people walked on country, speaking

language, obeying lore.

When white men came, and with them the telegraph poles, the white man's laws, camels, Christianity, horses, railways, sugar, booze, money, pianos and diseases, the people first thought the spirits had solidified. They were astonished by the white men's ugliness, their skin as pale as cooked iguana, their eyes as blue as the sky, and they were appalled by the smell. White men smelled of death to them.

Reinventing himself was exactly what Hank Jefferson needed to do. His marriage was on the brink of collapse after his career as the financial manager of a large corporation in Sydney had ended. He was not short of money as he had received a handsome golden handshake and had saved ever since he married Bettina, who was German and exceptionally well-organised.

His trips around Australia, following all the Masters Games and taking part in the tennis and running competitions, had not brought him the clarity he had sought; neither had his trips around the world running marathons. Hank needed an answer to the question of what to do next. Of who to be. The arrogant, short-fused manager's attitude he had made his own did not do much for him now; neither did the sharp suits, the starched shirts and the vertically striped ties. The trips rather depressed him, as they had confirmed what he already knew and dreaded: that he was getting older.

During one of the Masters Game events, he had visited Alice Springs. All the hotels had been booked, and he had ended up renting a private room for two weeks in the house of a single mother who had resembled what's-her-name-again, that stand-up comedian from Alice Springs. Sport had played a secondary role, as he had thrown himself into drinking, smoking, and having sex with the strapped-for-cash woman who was not Fiona what-was-her-name-again, ah yeah, Fiona McLaughlin, but looked a lot like her. She was more curvy than Fiona and generous, with a hint of Maori blood, and she had brought light and warmth to his despair with her throaty laugh, her cheerful dresses, her lace bras, her dusty CDs of didgeridoo music and her art collection. She had told him about her love for Alice Springs, the town of painters. Her house was filled with Aboriginal art and artefacts that fetched outrageous prices in the town's many galleries. But no matter how strapped for cash, she would not part with her art collection.

Her kid had been staying with a friend during the Masters Games, so he never met it, but colourful toys were lying around. The toys had made him want to weep for some reason, and the woman had stroked his back when he drunkenly told her that Bettina could not have children. He had given the woman some extra money when he paid her the rent after two weeks. She had accepted it gratefully and cheerfully and told him she would buy herself a couple of paper lamps at Kmart.

"At Kmart?" he had asked, surprised.

"Yes, honey. We in Alice Springs all wear the same Kmart clothes, haven't you noticed? We also furnish our houses almost identically. We do not have a choice, do we now? They have nice, cheap lamps in Kmart at the moment. You never know how long that will last."

She had come home with three large lamps on stands made out of rice paper and then had cooked him a goodbye dinner of kangaroo steak, sweet potato, carrot and onion while he had unpacked and set up the lamps.

"Where do you want them?" he had asked, a lamp in each hand, and he felt insanely happy for a second or two.

"There, there and there," she had pointed, and the lamps had blended into her messy interior like landed fish released back into the sea. When he turned them on, her interior glowed with an inner light that could not be explained.

She had used generous amounts of herbs that made the room smell of a French country hotel; thyme, rosemary, and garlic, which she had picked from her prickly garden. They had eaten at her bare wooden table decorated with an empty jam jar holding a bouquet of unruly mint, kangaroo paw and eucalyptus twigs.

The lamps had shed a golden light on their sins of

wine, cigarettes and sex. She had put on her high heels and some lipstick, and he had taken her from behind while she was bent over the table, between the dirty plates and glasses. Her bright pink Kmart slip, which she hadn't bothered to remove and that now cupped her haunches tightly, drove him wild as he looked down to where their bodies locked. He lifted her light green cotton Kmart skirt to get an even better view and came explosively and far too early. She then demanded that he lick her to liberation, and he had done so eagerly, while fingering her at the same time. He had never done that to Bettina or any other woman and did not understand where he found the technique, but the woman was grateful. They shared a cigarette afterwards.

"Your chin is still wet," she had said, and he had not felt ashamed.

The following day he had sheepishly asked for an iron to smoothen his shirt and shaved his beard off. She had watched him in the mirror, sitting on a high stool behind him.

He had sobbed clumsily into her fragrant armpit for a minute when they said goodbye at the town's small airport that she had driven him to in her dusty old Nissan Terrano that smelled of diesel.

His chest had produced a single dry sob as he was lifted into the vast blue sky. He had been surprised by how unmoved she was by their separation, but then, he thought, she might do this every two years, during the Masters Games. Rent out the room for cash to a not-too-young, not-too-old male and have some fun at the same time. Buy herself something nice at Kmart afterwards. Get on with her life with her kid.

When Bettina picked him up at Sydney Airport four hours later in her dark blue BMW, he noticed how thin her lips were, how bony her frame; and although he had been away for two weeks, there was not a whole lot of talking in the traffic jam to Homebush Bay, where they owned a large apartment.

Bettina knew, he knew, instantly. She had seen it in his eyes when their eyes met when he stepped into the arrivals area. He had gone astray. She never said anything about it. But he knew that she knew and she knew that he knew that she knew. Their silences deepened and weren't comfortable. Their bodies seemed unsuited to being in one room or one car, let alone in one bed.

"Haf you vigured aut vot you vont?," she asked him one evening, when he was leafing through Richard Trudgen's *Why Warriors Lie Down and Die*, and she was reading Eckhart Tolle; and he answered: "No."

"Try dis." She handed him *The Power of Now*. "No thanks." He handed her the book back.

"You did not even hav a look," she said. "No vunder you don't know vot you vont. You will not vaind it if you don't look for it."

He tried to tell her about the art collection — the shimmering oranges and blue-greens, like the desert itself, the clumsy but exquisite pointillism — without ever mentioning the woman. He showed her the pictures from a catalogue he had picked up in a gallery in Alice Springs, but the paintings looked flat and meaningless on their glossy paper in the grey light of their apartment. They seemed bleak, like wild parrots in a cage; meaningless, like delicate flowers torn from their stems; pathetic, like tropical fish in a tank, out of place, like a dusty Outback man in Sydney.

"Let's go to some Aboriginal Art galleries. We never go out together anymore," he said to Bettina.

"Okay," she agreed reluctantly.

Walking around in the galleries, looking at the large, expensive canvasses, he was in the grip of that strange evasive sense of hope that he had experienced in the house of the woman in Alice Springs. The paintings reminded him of her cheerful warmth, and of the heat and the redness of the deserts. He was overcome with a longing to go back.

"Bettina," he said, almost breathlessly, "let's go to Alice Springs."

She raised her right eyebrow. "Why?"

He gestured around him clumsily, indicating the paintings around them. "For, eh, this."

She shrugged. "It's, eh, nice, but to go all the way to

Alice Springs for it, no. Shall we have a coffee?"

During that coffee, he was tempted to confess, to tell Bettina all about the woman. But when he was on the verge of opening his mouth, she said: "I wouldn't mind going to Ayers Rock. I haven't seen that yet."

He nodded. Bettina wanted to go to Alice Springs! That was progress. He didn't know why, but it was.

"It is called Uluru," he said.

"What?"

"Ayers Rock is now called Uluru."

"Why?" She asked.

"It's what Aboriginal people call it."

"You are all ret in the face," Bettina remarked.

"I'm feeling a bit feverish," he said.

"Ah," said Bettina. Her eyes looked through the window, following a woman and a child walking by.

"Then you should go to bed, ja?" she concluded once the woman and child had disappeared from view.

"Yeah," he said. "I'm exhausted."

"Exhausted from what?" she demanded.

"Jesus, leave me alone," he snapped, "just exhausted."

She raised her large pale hands: "Okay, I didn't say anything."

He suppressed a strong urge to hit her. He suddenly hated her, hated their life together. Her pale hands, her stupid accent, her silent suffering about not having a child, her senior HR job, their immaculate cars, their spotless apartment, his shirts perfectly arranged on their wooden hangers, like an army of limp soldiers. Then the stainless-steel kitchen, where they never cooked any food to speak of, where they merely reheated takeaways in the microwave.

"Let's buy some herbs in pots for the kitchen," he said.

"Why?" she asked, "We never cook."

Now it was his turn to raise his hands in defence. "Just a thought, not important."

She grabbed her lime-green designer bag and stood up. "Let's go."

He walked behind her, looking at her slim body in the expensive pearl-coloured linen dress, her flat grey sandals, her toenails painted pearl to match. He opened the door for her.

"Thank you," she said.

He felt ashamed and he didn't know why.

Once he was in bed at the Homebush Bay apartment, she brought him water with ice in a pitcher and an empty glass, Tiger Balm and a thermometer.

He guiltily indulged in the images he had filed away carefully in his brain for later use – the Kmart slip, the cherry-red lipstick, the pink lace bra, the rounded white flesh... He was hard and began masturbating. His erection was soon holding up the blanket like a tent pole, and he pumped it feverishly as soon as Bettina had left the room. She returned just after he had climaxed. He was slightly out of breath.

"Jesus, ja, you have fever," she said, and placed a cool hand on his forehead. "You should take a Panadene Forte."

"Yes, please," he whispered. *Anything to block out this feeling of guilt*, he thought, swallowing four tablets.

Imagine this: you and your family are walking country, speaking language, obeying lore. It is hot and dry. You are naked and barefoot and as you are carrying stuff in both hands, you have to use your chin to point at things. You are used to shouting over large distances. You use sign language if the distance is too large. You have lost several babies and toddlers. But now your family has grown too big, say three or four teenage children, and there's not enough food and water around for such a large group. It would be best if you parted with your children, and send them into another direction because they eat and drink a lot. You put your gear down in the shade of a low mulga tree.

Pointing into one direction, you say: "We go this way".

Point into the opposite direction, you say: "You go that way."

There are no tracks, just a huge stretch of barren land with blue mallee shrubs, wattle, kiji, and mulga. Here and there, a gum tree. That is the point where you say goodbye to your children and you hope they will be all right. That's how it is. You hope you will bump into them later. You will get together for ceremonies perhaps. That's all you can do. Country is vast and relentless and chances are that you will perish or they will perish before you ever meet again, and there is nothing you can do about it. That is the way of the lore.

If your parents are still with you, this is the point where they will offer to stay behind. They know they have become a burden. They will climb a hill and wait for death to take them to the land of spirits and ancestors, back to the Dreamtime. You will return to find their corpses. You will tie them with vines to a large piece of bark. You will place the package of bark and flesh in a gum tree. And you will leave it there to be eaten by the split-tail eagles, the itchy grubs and the flies. You will move on, from waterhole to waterhole. That is the lore. You have taught your children this. Your parents have taught you this. You have no say in it. Your duty is to walk country.

"Jesus, it's hot," said Bettina, when they stepped on the tarmac of the landing strip of Alice Springs. "They should put some shade trees in here."

People in light-coloured safari clothes and wide-rimmed Akubra hats passed them and made their way to the exit. Bettina hastily took her Ray-Bans from their case and put them on.

Hank stretched in the dry air, reaching with his hands to the blue sky. "Look how cute these little white clouds are," he said, sniffing the air that smelled of dust and diesel.

She was not used to him saying things like that and looked at him doubtfully. Was he serious? "Let's go."

Bettina had brought fruit for both of them in the Northern Territory; they left it in the border bin, but not after a little scene by Bettina, and walked between the row of banners, marking the way to the exit.

Welcome to Mbantua. Please respect our land. The people of the Caterpillar Dreaming welcome you. The words flapped in the hot wind.

The taxi driver was Indian.

"Will there be many snakes?" Bettina asked, looking at the barren redness outside.

"Oh, yes," the driver said enthusiastically. "Hazardous ones. And spiders too."

"Look," said Hank, pointing at the Alice Springs welcome sign carved out of the red rock.

"What?"

"Well, isn't that beautiful?"

She looked at him sharply again.

"You want a photograph there?" the driver asked, breaking abruptly.

"Sure," said Hank, and handed him his iPhone. Once in front of the enormous sign, he put his arm around

Bettina. She leaned into him a little. They both smiled. Hank stamped onto the red dirt with his new desert boots. He felt as if the land belonged to him, or rather if he belonged to the land.

"Will you give us a little tour of the town before you drop us off, please?" Bettina requested the driver.

"I will do my best, madam. I have just arrived here myself."

"What were you in India?" asked Hank.

"A professor of Astronomy, Sir."

"So why are you a taxi driver now?"

"The Australian government does not recognise my degrees, Sir."

"I know all about that," said Bettina. "I had to study all over again. That's despite the German educational system being much better than the Australian."

"The same counts for India, Madam."

"Stupid Certificates Four and Diplomas, I would do them in a weekend. They should realise that."

"Me too, Madam. Very easy." The taxi driver giggled. "Tedious but easy. Well, this is Heavitree Gap."

"Vocational training, instead of scientific education. It should not be like that, but it is," Bettina said, unable to hide her disgust.

Sharp red rocks towered on both sides of the road.

"The gap was carved through the centuries by the Todd River." The driver pointed to a sandy riverbed with trees growing in it. Bettina looked at it with disapproval. Hank suddenly found she looked like a parrot, with her large, judgemental nose.

"Look at the light. Isn't it beautiful?"

Bettina seemed confused by everything he said. "What light?"

"Are those houses?" asked Bettina, pointing.

"Yes, Ma'am."

"God!"

"You might want to visit the Reptile Centre, the Royal Flying Doctors and the Old Gaol, with the Women's Hall of Fame." The taxi driver drew their attention to several buildings erected around a large grassy area where groups of Aboriginal people were sitting, surrounded by bags.

"What are these people sitting around doing there?"

"They have no work, Madam. They drink. Pay no attention to them."

"There are hundreds of them; how can you not pay attention to them? Look, there they're sitting in the middle of the road."

"They are unfortunates, Ma'am, pay no attention and you will have a good time."

"How can you not look at them? And those houses look like sheds."

"They are very expensive, Ma'am, the houses."

"How expensive?"

"Between three hundred and four hundred thousand

for the smallest ones, Madam."

"And the rents?"

"About six hundred and fifty a week for a three-bedroom, Madam."

"That's the same as in Sydney. Why is it so expensive?"

"Because there is no land, Madam."

"No land? We're in the middle of nowhere!"

"It all belongs to the Aboriginal people, Ma'am."

"So why don't they build, instead of..." she was looking for the right way to say it, "instead of sitting around getting pissed."

"They can't get mortgages, Ma'am."

"Why is that?"

"Because they were given the land for life, Ma'am. The bank cannot claim it."

"Great!" said Bettina, leaning back in disgust, "so where do these people sleep?"

"In the riverbed, Ma'am."

"I beg your pardon?"

"This here is the CBD," said the taxi driver.

"This is the centre?"

"There's the Mall. They are renovating it now, so few shops are open. There's Woollies, Coles, Kmart, Ma'am."

"Are they renovating that cute little mall?' asked Hank. "What a pity. It was so relaxing there." He felt an acute sense of loss. He had walked there with the woman, and now it would never be the same again. He looked for signs to aid his faded memory.

"Since when do you find little things 'cute', and since when do you say 'relaxing'?" asked Bettina. "Cute little clouds, cute little mall...I think it is ugly as sin, to tell the truth."

"Wait until you see the galleries," said Hank, hopeful.

*

It was very early in the morning. Linda Van Halen was humming softly. Standing behind the counter, she looked at a series of extremely small paintings from a relatively unknown community in the Simpson Desert. The community had only forty-six inhabitants who spoke a language that had never been written down. There were only seven children among them.

Linda was well-groomed and looked precisely like a gallery owner should: a medium-long asymmetrical bob, the fringe extremely short, a prominent pair of designer glasses with orange accents on the temples, and a vintage dress with a fifties print - green bottles on a beige background, with here and there an orange line; comfortable yet high-heeled orange shoes; and jewellery from European museums' contemporary art shops.

She was absorbed in the series of paintings. The

smallest was no bigger than a book of matches; the largest, the size of a cigar box. She was sure children had not painted them. They were the work of an adult male.

She turned the largest one around and smiled when she saw it had been painted on the wooden lid of an old cigar box. She gave a slight shiver, just as she had when discovering Kudditji Kngwarreye, the Rothko of the Red Centre. But these mini paintings were nothing like the mysterious colour fields of Kudditji Kngwarreye. They were naive landscapes showing little figures riding brumbies, children in colourful clothes, camp dogs; and all, even the bright blue sky and orange desert sand, painted with a two-hair brush. Here and there, the sky bore little white clouds...

As usual, when she encountered something unique, Linda hesitated to put prices on them, wanting to keep them for herself. It was, she knew, a fleeting sentiment. She would cherish them for a couple of weeks as if they were hers, then something else would come along, and she would get all excited about that, and that was when she would price them; when she had disengaged from them naturally. She re-wrapped them carefully in the rough paper they had been packed in and carried them to the back room.

While she was walking through her gallery, she breathed in deeply to have a sense of inhaling the vibrant colours and shapes that were everywhere. She loved her gallery, with its ample, airy space and metal staircases; especially in the early morning, when hardly anyone was out and about, it had a silent magic.

There seemed to be an unusual scent in the air. She tried to pinpoint what it was.

She had some big early George Ward paintings and a few very sparse Walala paintings. She avoided the leaf-painting Mbatjabi family – they were in all other galleries anyway – and concentrated on the old desert men, whose style would soon be gone forever.

It was quiet in the Mall because the renovations discouraged customers from coming in large numbers. Businesses around her gallery were failing at an alarming rate, but Linda, who was not reliant on walk-in clients, held on. She sold her paintings to big collectors worldwide. They made appointments before they visited. The work she exhibited was usually large and suited to corporate display: vast firms' hallways and board rooms. Her clients also included the owners of large hotels. For the occasional tourist or for long-term locals wishing to add to their ever-growing collections of Indigenous art and artefacts, she had a fine display of indigenous jewellery, woven baskets and smaller paintings.

*

At four in the morning, Blue McCallas woke up to the alarm on his phone. It rang like an old metal alarm clock. He cursed while looking for his glasses to be able to turn the damn' thing off. Wearing only his glasses, he slouched into the shower and let the hot water beat onto his fat back until the dark mood of the night began to fade. It was already too hot for the ceiling fans to relieve the heat, so he turned on the swampy. The motor came to life noisily. He dressed quickly and absent-mindedly, checking with his thick fingers in the back pocket of his jeans for the key of the Troopy, then in the breast pocket of his RM Williams shirt for his wad of cash. He shoved another roll of cash into the side of one of his Cuban-heeled Santa Fe's and looked around for his Akubra. It was sitting upside-down on the table, the leather sweatband heavily stained. He knocked the top of the hat around a bit until the dent was just right and put it on while grabbing a litre pack of iced coffee from the fridge. He drank thirstily while he set the front door alarm and walked to the driveway.

He thought about the many break-ins by kids. They had no respect for their Elders any longer. He'd show them a lesson or two if he caught one or more in his house. He'd drive them fifty K out of town and have them walk back. That'd teach them.

The chick from Byron Bay had washed the Troopy. He'd given her fifty dollars for it. What was her name again? Sharon, that's right. "Byron," she kept calling it.

He grinned and wondered how long it would take to get her into his bed, this chick from Byron. His being not a vegetarian might slow the process, but then, if he took her to his land... That usually did the trick with these hippy types. And the fact that he was Aboriginal. She had promised to help him with the fencing.

The Troopy was nice and clean inside. He turned the key and that engine sprang to life with a roar. Blue roared too, and grinned. He loved the sound of a well-oiled Toyota diesel motor.

He patted the dash. "Good girl."

It was still dark. Slowly he steered the Troopy onto the deserted North Stuart Highway, in the direction of the town. It had been dry for a long time and the kangaroos were everywhere, looking for water. A big one jumped at his headlights within seconds, but it was easy to avoid. A bit further down the road, a camel was lying lazily in the middle of the tarmac. Blue slammed the horn, but the beast did not even move its ears. He had to steer off the road and around it, careful not to upset it. It was a bull, and a mad bull camel is no fun to deal with in the early morning. Blue imagined being crushed by the stump hanging from the shabby beast's daggy belly. It was about time someone built a dog food factory and start shooting the filthy animals in big numbers, he thought. They were coming that close to town now and lying in the middle of the road, acting like royalty.

With the first hint of morning light colouring the West MacDonnell ranges a deep purple, Blue unclipped his Ray-Bans from the sunscreen and put them on. Now he was complete: the Akubra and the Ray-Bans would not come off for the rest of the day.

Still driving slowly, he peered into the flaming half-dark on both roadsides. His Ray Bans intensified the oranges and reds that now glowed on the horizon. Hitting a roo or a camel was one thing; hitting a drunk was another. This town was an invitation to being sent to jail because of hitting a drunk. There were so many drunks that not hitting one in your lifetime in Alice Springs could be called a miracle. Blue snorted, almost sobbed momentarily. Bloody losers, bloody disgraces to their race. Blue was Aboriginal, but he was not a drunk, and neither was he unemployed. Well, he was, sort of. He operated in two worlds, the white one and the black one. This was kind of symbolic, for it was how he looked as well. Blue was Aboriginal in all ways possible: the broad nose, the wide face, the shy mouth, the thin calves... except that Blue's skin was white and his eyes blue. That was why his mum had called him Blue. His mum, who could be found at the Casino behind a poky machine at any hour of the day or night, was as black as they come. She seemed to be made of leather. He had never met his dad, but had heard from his mum that he was Irish. Had he, Blue, as a half-caste, been of the previous generation, he would most likely have been taken away from his family and put into an institution. His mum had been terrified of that happening. During her childhood, children had been stolen around Alice Springs, and also in the rest of the country. According to his mum, the stealing of children went on well into the 1970s, although not so openly as before. She had made sure he blended in and never attracted any attention. He had become a master at blending in wherever he went. Blue was an art dealer of sorts. The darker side of his business dealings he preferred to undertake in the very early mornings, when drunks were most desperate for booze.

There were street lights along the highway now he was nearing the town. Dark silhouettes, men and women and even the occasional child, were staggering towards the town. He scanned the fragmented groups for hints of white rolled-up canvasses. Bingo. A teenage girl was holding one. She was very drunk. He slowed and rolled his window down. A hot whiff of wind, booze and body odour hit him.

"Good morning, sister," he cried.

The girl turned towards the car.

"Can I see the painting?"

She unrolled it and showed it to him. It was large, and it was a beauty.

"How much?" he asked, his face neutral.

"Three hundred bucks," she said.

He pretended to drive off.

"Brother," she yelled. "What about two hundred?"

He braked abruptly. "What about some booze?"

"What have you got, Bro?"

"Get in the car."

She did not hesitate and slipped onto the passenger seat.

He took an esky from the back seat and opened it. "Whisky, port, rum, the best, you choose."

"The lot," she said.

"You can have two," he said. "Put the painting in the back seat. Do you have a bag?"

"No."

He gestured at her feet. "Coles bags there, take one."

She carelessly threw the painting on the back seat, snatched the plastic bag from the floor and took a bottle of whisky and a bottle of port.

"Thanks, Bro." She opened the door and slid into the half-dark.

He looked at his watch. He needed to reach the dry riverbed before it was fully light. He sped through town while keeping one eye on each staggering group in case they had paintings.

He parked his car as close as possible to the Todd River bridge and waited.

Half an hour later, his esky was empty, and so was his Santa Fe, but the money in his breast pocket was still there. On the back seat were five paintings and twelve long strings of painted beads held together with strands of human hair. He threw a blanket over the loot.

At the back of Van Halen's gallery they were already loading and unloading stuff when he passed. Bloody Van Halen! She had never bought anything from him. It was not as if she did not have the money.

"Mister McCallas, you don't need me and I don't need you," she had once said, "Let's leave it at that, if that's okay with you."

"Rich bitch," he said. She was monopolising the business more and more. Almost all the big buyers went through her gallery nowadays. And how long had she been here altogether? Ten years at the most? A blow-in. A white one too. A woman. A single woman who did not seem to need a man. Probably one of the many lesbians that gathered here. But he had not seen her in those circles either. Van Halen seemed to do nothing but work. While everyone was going bust, she was still going strong. What was her fucking secret? Had not the bottom fallen out of the Aboriginal art trade a couple of years ago? Had not nearly all galleries disappeared from Gregory Terrace that year? The ones in the Mall were hanging on by their fingernails, but Van Halen seemed untouched by it all. Every morning she was high-heeling herself through her gallery, turning this light on, adjusting that painting, click, clack, on the polished tiles, her make-up outspoken, dress weird, hair buoyant, pity that she cut that fringe, and the lipstick was always the wrong colour.... Van Halen was irritating.

A bloke was trolleying crates in and out of a van. Big crates too. Probably Western Desert stuff or Top End. Who was her go-between? He wondered for the millionth time. She did not go through the art centres, that much he knew.

He turned the Troopy around and went for his morning coffee to the Chiffley's Resort, just over the bridge, where David Damport was already waiting for him in the parking lot.

"What have you got?" Damport asked, without saying good morning. He was a tall, handsome man of Afghan descent.

"Top of the morn to you too," Blue replied, while removing the blanket on the back seat.

Damport unrolled the paintings, making sure they did not stick out of the car; he fingered the strings of beads. "On real hair, eh?"

"Yup."

"How much you want for the lot?"

"Five thousand."

"Two and a half."

"Four thousand eight hundred, nothing less."

"Get outa here, mate."

This continued for another two minutes until they settled and shook hands. It was their usual morning dance.

"What time, where?" asked Damport.

"In an hour at my shed," said Blue, already walking into the direction of the terrace at the pool, longing for his coffee.

"Good morning, Mister Blue, how are you today?" said Tomiko, the waitress in black. "The usual?"

Blue smiled widely and shyly. "Yes, sweetheart, please."

A bit later, the Japanese girl arrived with his flat white in-a-cup-not-a-mug, with two tiny mint chocolates, separately wrapped. He looked at her little figure as she walked away. Compact as an egg, he thought. Amazing how many Japanese and Koreans there were in Alice lately. First, it was the Indians, arriving in hordes; the men were the taxi drivers now, the women nurses. The Japanese and Koreans worked in hospitality and tourism. The latest blow-ins were from Africa and were as black as his mother. None of these groups had any interest in indigenous art. They were sending their hard-earned money home instead, Blue guessed. The last thing their families needed was art, let alone Indigenous art from the Australian Red Centre. That was something for Northern Europe and America, the rich from the East Coast of Australia, and the local collectors. They were getting a good deal, the locals, because once the art reached the coasts of Australia, it had already doubled in price, if not tripled. It doubled or tripled again after an overseas trip to Europe or the USA. These regions were in a recession now. India, China and Korea were the rising economies, but they were not interested in the awkward paintings of the people of Central Australia.

*

Bettina and Hank went to Linda's van Halen's gallery before they departed to Uluru by tour bus.

"What a weird name for a gallery: Fafaf," said Bettina.

"It was the name of my dog. He died shortly before I opened the gallery," Linda explained.

Hank was enthusiastically walking around and talking Linda. She showed him some extremely small paintings. He was standing close to the gallery holder with her asymmetrical outfit and stupid fringe, Bettina observed, which irritated the shit out of Bettina. This was the woman he'd had sex with, she suddenly realised. She's smelled her on his clothes, seen her in his eyes... This was the W in his contact list on his phone. They were intimately admiring the stupid little paintings, their heads close together above the counter. They laughed delightedly at the "cute little clouds" in the sky. What the hell had gone wrong with Hank? Could he not see through the scam that this art clearly was?

"Did you know that lady?" she asked while walking to the hotel, where the tour bus would pick them up.

Hank looked her straight in the eyes.

"No," he said.

"Yes, you did!" she poked him in his ribs playfully.

"No, honestly!"

They were now at the Rock.

Bettina still thought it was stupid to call it "Uluru", but whenever she said "Ayers Rock" she was corrected. What was wrong with those people? Had they gone native? The bus driver, the guide, the other travellers…? They all seemed hell-bent on calling the rock "Uluru." They weren't Aboriginal, so why call it Uluru?

Yulara was the only place where they could sleep, it turned out, and it was a tourist trap like no other. Tourists occupied the whole village; there were no normal houses, only hotels.

Bettina and Hank had booked the most expensive hotel, outside the village, a series of Eco-tents erected on wooden platforms and furnished like hotel rooms. Shiny four-wheel drives were randomly parked in the sand. Hank and Bettina were waiting for their star-lit dinner, sitting on the wooden deck before their tent. A couple of the four-wheel drives had their lights set on high-beam to assist the waiters in white clothes who were putting damask table clothes on trestle tables in the sand and laying out silver cutlery, white crockery and crystal glasses.

Hank was watching a documentary on his iPad about Geoffrey Burdon and the Papunya painters in the 70s. Bettina was reading Eckhardt Tolle.

Along with about a thousand other people, they had just witnessed the sun setting on the Rock. The Rock had gone dark purple, then red, then orange, then back to purple again. In the space of an hour, these various stages had been photographed at least thirty thousand times.

"One might as well hire a personal traveller,' Bettina joked.

"Huh," said Hank, not understanding.

"Instead of a personal shopper, someone who travels for you, so you don't have to get out and do it yourself."

"Oh," said Hank. "Ha ha."

"But the Rock is beautiful in the sunset, I must admit," said Bettina.

"It is as if the light comes from inside," Hank remarked.

"It's just evening sunlight reflected off the stone," said Bettina. "There's a lot of red in the evening light that reflects off the different angles of the stone. There's red in the surrounding soil too. That might be part of it as well."

"You can almost feel how old this landscape is, don't you think?" said Hank, picking up a small rock from the well-trodden dust.

"I don't know about that," answered Bettina. "But

you can see it. The flatness of it, and the round shapes of the rocks. No recent volcanic activity...."

"In the early seventies, I camped here," said Hank. "But that was over after a dingo stole the Chamberlain baby from the campgrounds."

Bettina was not really listening to what he was saying. She nodded vaguely. Had she never heard of the most famous court case there had ever been in Australia? Didn't she know that half the nation had been driving around with stickers on their cars saying *The Dingo Did It*, the other half with stickers saying *The Dingo Is Innocent*? She was so absorbed in her German culture that she rarely showed interest in Australian history. Hank had tried to tell her this several times.

"Australia is a young country with a shallow culture," she had answered. "Germany is very old and has a deep culture. Which would you choose if you were me? Eh?"

He still tried to interest her in the Geoffrey Burdon documentary he was watching. This man was extraordinary; he had first encouraged Aboriginal people to paint.

"Their paintings would not last because they were painted on the body or in the sand," he said, "Burdon changed all that."

Bettina nodded vaguely again, not looking up from her Eckhardt Tolle book. This one bore the title *A New Earth*.

"He made them paint on the walls of the school of Papunya and let them tell the stories connected with the images. He wrote these stories down."

"Hmmm," she said.

"How can you be so uninterested?" he wondered.

"It happened in the seventies," she said. "That's not what we call history."

By "we" she meant Germans, Hank assumed. "But Burdon was revealing a sixty-thousand-year-old history there," he tried again.

Bettina looked up from her book. "But nothing changed in those sixty thousand years, did it? They started off naked and they were still naked at the beginning of this century."

Hank did not know how to respond to this. He knew she was wrong but didn't know why or how. He experienced his familiar irritation and then disappointment.

"Listen, I don't find those paintings that interesting," she said, and looked at him.

"I know you don't. But can't you see how they work, I mean: how they work here in this light, under these skies?"

She shook her head. "Nope. Overpriced shit, that's what it is."

Hank felt pained, as if he were the one she had put down, not the paintings of Aboriginal people.

"To tell you the truth, I would rather not be found dead with one of these paintings on my walls."

Hank sighed, feeling wounded, and thought about the woman in Alice. How she had genuinely loved the place she lived in and the art she was surrounded by.

"I've read that this art industry is corrupt," continued Bettina. "And that it's a threat to non-Aboriginal artists. They claim they've invented dotting. What nonsense! The French had pointillism when the Aboriginals were still living in trees."

Hank wanted to reply that Aboriginal people had never lived in trees, but he was overcome by the sudden exhaustion that Bettina caused in him.

An old-fashioned cowbell started ringing near the tables. The lights of the four-wheel drives were dimmed, the white tablecloths gleamed, and guests were making their way to the tables, stumbling a bit in the dark.

"It's dinner time, I think," said Bettina and carefully placed a bookmark between the pages of her book.

"Wow," said Hank when he looked up at the sky. "Look at these stars."

Bettina gave him a sharp look again. "Yes, they are stars. The same stars as everywhere else."

Once seated, Bettina folded her hands under her chin and rested her head on them. Hank thought she looked like a Picasso painting. All out of wack.

She looked at Hank while a waiter poured champagne into their glasses.

"Hank," she said, when the waiter was gone.

Here it comes, thought Hank. God help me.

"Why don't we separate for a while? Go our own ways. I need that. Don't you?"

Did he hear that correctly? He stared at her.

"What do you think?" she urged.

"Well, erm, yes, I would like that too," he admitted, and he felt an overwhelming sense of relief.

"What would you like to do?" she asked.

"I would like to stay here, in the Red Centre, and start an art gallery," he replied.

What the hell am I saying? he thought.

"See?" said Bettina.

"What?"

"That woman has you mesmerised."

"No, Bettina, really!"

Should he tell her about her mistake? That it was another woman he had been unfaithful with? A much more down-to-earth woman.

"What would you do?" he said instead.

"I would return to Germany for a while," she said. "I'm homesick. I want to be with my parents for a while. They are getting old."

Hank nodded, stunned.

"You might never come back," he said after a long silence.

"I might, I might not," she said and smiled. It had been a long time since he'd seen her smile.

"You are a terrific woman," he said, suddenly convinced that he meant this wholeheartedly. "I've always known that."

"No, you haven't," she said. "But that's all right."

"So, where do we go from here?" Hank stammered.

"You stay here, and I go home," she replied. "Simple as that."

"Okay," he said slowly.

She lifted her glass. "Goodbye, my love," she said.

Hank did not speak but lifted his glass slowly and clinked it to hers. The crystal sang in the clean air.

"Crystal glasses, "she remarked, "classy! Listen, I'll fly out of here back to Sydney. I'll lock up the apartment and go to Germany from there," she continued.

Hank gulped down his drink. "What about your job?"

"I've already arranged that."

What? She had been planning this all along! Hank felt some anger but decided not to act on it. He smiled instead.

"I loved the manager in you," Bettina said. "Not that arty guy you want to be now."

"I see," he replied.

"I miss that crisply dressed big-headed man," Bettina continued. "But I realise that man is gone."

Hank thought about that for a while. "Yes, that man is gone," he said.

Bettina did not say anything about his affair, although

he knew she knew and she knew that he knew that she knew. He found this a bit unsettling. It was unlike Bettina. Bettina always had the last word and dug deep. It used to drive him mad. Now he almost wished she would interrogate him so that he could confess and correct her mistake.

*

Damport was already waiting outside Blue's shed when Blue parked his Troopy, raising a cloud of dust.

"Come with me," he said to Hank Jefferson, who was occupying the front seat.

A group of Aboriginal people were standing at the roller doors, shouting at each other. They were wearing their usual clothes: the men dirty RM Williams jeans and Santa Fe's, RM Williams shirts and broad-brimmed black Akubra hats, the women long floral skirts from Vinnies and oversized T-shirts. No bras. Nearly all the women were fat. Most of the men were lean, mean and tall. Snotty-nosed children sat in the dirt. A couple of camp dogs were lying around scratching themselves. Old dusty Holdens and Ford Falcon station wagons were untidily parked everywhere.

Blue scanned the crowd to assess the general

atmosphere quickly.

"Today women and children only!" he shouted, opening the roller door with a remote control and pushing the men away roughly. "No, no, no dogs allowed."

"Come," he said to Damport and Hank while the women were flocking into the shed and taking their places at their paintings on the concrete floor.

Blue closed the roller door and the racket was instantly gone. Only the noise of badly starting cars penetrated through the roller door, and then that too was gone.

The women opened their acrylic paint pots; some dipped sticks in and began making dots, some had brushes and painted leaves with one stroke, others painted bold abstracts; some had a child sitting at their side.

"Ah," said Blue while they walked to a small office in the corner of the shed, "I love that moment when silence descends. Outside, their lives are in chaos, they never know what will happen to them next, but here they can concentrate. They love it. As long as I keep the men and the women separated, all is well. The screaming will start when I release them at five this afternoon as soon as they step out through that door."

Damport did not bother to reply. He took a thick roll of cash from his pocket, peeled off some notes and placed them on the desk.

"You feed them as well?"

"Only the women and the children. I built them

showers too."

"You're too good. Here, count it."

Blue quickly counted the cash, rolled it up, stuck it in his Santa Fe and gave Damport the keys to the Troopy.

"Take them all, but leave the keys on the front seat, will ye?"

"No problem," said Damport, ducking out from under the roller door that Blue had just opened.

"I'll see you around."

Blue quickly checked that all Aboriginal men had gone, then closed the roller door. He took two loaves of bread out of the beaten-up fridge in the office, two roasted chickens, and cartons of iced coffee and milk, and put it all on the only table in the shed.

"Breakfast is ready," he said.

The women scrambled to their feet and lined up at the table shyly.

"Children first," said Blue. "No, no coffee for you, little one, it's milk for you."

The boy, about nine, protested, but Blue looked at him sternly.

"I said 'no'."

"After breakfast, you all take a shower, understand?" Blue said. "You lot stink!"

The women giggled.

"I mean it," said Blue. "And this arvo we go to Vinnies to buy some new clothes for you mob. The ones you're wearing now can go in the washing machine, you hear me? I can't have you mob stinking up my shed."

More giggling followed. Some women hid their faces behind their hands. They sat on the floor to eat and then returned to their paintings.

"Feel free to look through these paintings there," Blue said to Hank, who was sitting on the only chair in the room. Hank stood up and began handling the large stack of canvasses as if he were reading a giant book. Now and then, he pulled one out and put it aside.

"You go take a shower first," said Blue, helping an older woman to her feet. "And take that little one there with you. Make sure you get all the snot off her face. I don't want snot in my shed, you hear? No snot is better for all of us."

He squatted beside a woman who was wearing a bandanna with a floral print and looked at her painting. He moved his hand in circles above one corner of the painting.

"You're getting a bit slack in this area, Brenda, I'm going to black the whole corner out so that you can start anew, okay? Make sure you take breaks when you get tired. Drink a cuppa. Walk around a bit. Stretch your legs. I want the paintings to be strong, you understand?"

"You've gotta keep them on their toes," he said to Hank. "Have you found something you like?"

Hank gestured at the six paintings he had chosen

from the pile. "How much for these?"

"All Jay Gordons," said Blue. "You've got a good eye."

Blue leafed through them expertly. "Seventeen thousand for the lot."

"Can I pay by credit card?"

"No," said Blue bluntly.

"I have to go to town then and get cash."

"No problem," said Blue. You can take my car; the keys are on the driver's seat."

*

The woman stood in a long queue in the Westpac Bank. The building was far too cold. She was wearing a thin summer dress. Her cheerfully red polished toenails were lines in her dusty blue sandals. She hugged herself with her bare arms, protecting her chest from the icy cold wind the air-conditioner blasted at her. She wiggled her toes to keep her feet from freezing. She lifted her sunglasses to see how the queue was progressing. It was then that she saw Hank. He was at the counter, stuffing a large amount of cash in his wallet.

"Well, I'll be damned," she said when he walked past her while putting his wallet in his back pocket. "Hank Jefferson is back in town."

Hank jumped at the sound of his name. He saw the woman in her thin summer dress, her sunglasses propped in her messy hair, her nail-polished hands crossed in front of her sizable bosom, her sunburned feet in comfortable sandals, her coloured lips smiling, her brown eyes sparkling naughtily, and he realised that... he had forgotten her name.

"Hi," he said, scanning his memory feverishly.

"It's me, Caroline," she said, friendly, warm, and relaxed. "Remember me?"

"Caroline," he exclaimed, relieved. "I was going to call you."

"How are you?" she said.

"Fine. I mean good," said Hank. "I'm in a hurry. I'll call you a bit later today, okay?"

"Okay," she said. "Have dinner with a friend and me if you want. Seven at Chiffley's Resort. Dress nicely if you can."

"Oh, okay, yes, I would like that," he said. "Bye now, gotta run."

Walking towards Blue's Troopy, which was parked at the dry riverbed, he felt a surge of excitement. A complete business plan popped up in his head in less than a minute. He was good with numbers. He could make good money here.

He started the vehicle quickly and raced back to the industrial estate. This was going to work!

When he handed Blue the money in the office, just as Damport had done that morning, he felt as if he was part of a new mysterious world. A colourful world that produced more money with every brush stroke.

"Are there any sheds for rent around here that you know of?" he asked Blue.

"Plenty," said Blue. "What are you after?"

"Something like this," said Hank.

"Three doors down that way, around the corner" Blue said. "Eleven hundred a week. Exactly the same as this one. Six weeks' bond."

"Who does it belong to?"

"Me," said Blue, grinning. "I built three of them, all the same."

"I'll take it," said Hank. "From today, if that's possible."

"No problem," said Blue, producing a rental contract from a drawer. "It's pretty standard."

Hank glanced over the contract, signed it and put two piles of bills on the desk. "That's for the paintings; this is the bond and two weeks of rent. Count it."

Blue handed him a set of keys.

"That was quick."

"Yeah, I don't muck around," said Hank.

Blue, suddenly chatty, said: "What are you going to do there, mate. Start a new business?"

"Yeah, maybe," Hank said vaguely.

"What kind of business?" Blue wanted to know.

"Not sure yet," said Hank.

"You can't live there," Blue warned. "It's a shed. I've got a few houses for rent, if you're interested."

"Yeah, no problem," said Hank. "Is there a place that sells swags around here?"

"You're going to sleep there then?"

"No, man, don't worry."

"Over the road," said Blue. "They make them. You wanna rent a house?"

"Not yet. But where do I get a second-hand Cruiser or a Troopy or something?"

"I can help you with that," said Blue.

"Give me your number," said Hank, "I'll call you a bit later."

"Fourteen thousand for a Troopy like mine," said Blue.

"I'll call you," said Hank, suddenly sick of Blue. "Can I leave the paintings here?"

"I'll drive you to your shed with them," offered Blue.

"Okay, thanks."

In the car Blue tried to get Hank to talk about his plans, but Hank kept silent.

Blue helped Hank with the large roll of paintings at the roller door, waved and took off.

"See you around, pal."

Hank waved, absent-mindedly opening the roller door

with his new remote control. It opened with a screeching sound that echoed in the empty space behind. A sweltering heat escaped from the shed. Hank smelled fresh concrete. He looked around for the split system but found none. Three buttons on the wall indicated a swampy. He found a tap as well. He cranked the new swampy, which sprang to life noisily. Hank stood under the air duct to catch the water-cooled air.

Standing in the middle of the empty shed, he unzipped his iPad from its leather pocket and made a list:

Linen
Paints
Brushes
Sticks
Gesso
Car
Swag

He looked for Caroline's number in his phone. It was under 'W' for Woman.

He wondered if Bettina had ever gone through his phone. If she had, this was a suspicious entry. She could use it in a divorce if she was going to go that way. She had only talked of separation but was on her way to see her parents. God only knew what they would say about this separation and him losing his job and travelling around the world on his own. Was she really going back to Germany? And if so, was she ever coming back? And if not, what was she up to? Had she lied to him?

He edited the phone number entry. The number now came up as "Caroline". He dialled.

"Hey, it's me. How are you?"

"Good," she said. "What's up?"

"I want to buy paint, linen, Gesso, that sort of thing, is there a wholesaler in town?"

"Are you starting to paint? How exciting." She gave him an address. It was not far from his shed.

"I'll see you tonight," he said.

"Seven at Barra on Todd," she replied. "It's in the Chiffley's resort just over the bridge.

He walked to the paint wholesaler. His shirt was wet when he arrived. The saleswoman was attractive.

"Where can I buy a second-hand Toyota?" he asked, glancing around the warehouse that smelled of turpentine.

"This is a paint supply store," she replied.

"I know," he laughed. "I need acrylics, brushes, Gesso and linen. Lots. But I have no car yet to transport it."

"I can get you one," she said. "My mother has a Cruiser for sale. An eighties series," she added, "perfect for desert trips; no electronics.

"How much?"

"Eight thousand, I think. It needs some minor work done to it. Suspension, I think."

"I might be interested," Hank said while walking along the shelves. He lifted ten-litre buckets of paint and lined them up on the floor. "I would like a hundred litres of each of those. And Gesso. A hundred litres of red-brown and a hundred litres of black."

"Aren't you going to stretch the canvas before gesso-ing it?"

Hank thought about this. "Should I?"

"Yes," she said without hesitation. "You'll need stretching frames. Hardwood is the best."

She led him to a corner where pre-sawn frame parts were neatly stacked on racks. Hank concentrated on the most expensive ones and quickly made a large selection of sizes.

"What kind of canvas are you going to use?"

"No canvas," he said. "Linen. The best you have."

"That would be the Belgian linen," she said, leading him to a row of large rolls.

"Feel that." She rubbed the fabric with her thumb and middle finger.

He touched it and then bent over to smell it, as if he knew what he was doing.

He whistled through his teeth.

"Classy! Very handsome. A hundred metres of it, please."

Now it was her turn to whistle.

"You will have me out of stock in a single day," she

said.

"That's your problem," he replied. "A luxury problem, I'd say."

"I will have to call my husband," she said. "To help with the delivery."

Hank saw how she was trying to hide her excitement and was amused.

"Don't worry," he said, while he piled brushes and round wooden sticks on the counter, "I'll help you load the car up as soon as I have one. Do you have a box for these?"

She ran to the back of the warehouse and returned with a large cardboard box.

Women in Alice Springs were pretty; or pretty was not the right word. Handsome; the women were handsome here, thought Hank.

"You'll have to pay by credit card or cash," she warned. "I can't set you up with an account in one day."

"Credit card. I'll set up an account later," said Hank. "Can I go and look at that car today, do you think?"

"I'll ask my mum to drive it here," she said as she added up the figures on her electronic till. "I'll give you a ten per cent discount."

"On your mum's car?"

"No, on the painting materials, duh."

"Great!" said Hank.

Shortly after he had paid her probably the largest sum she had ever received, her mother appeared in the Cruiser.

Hank lifted the bonnet and inspected the engine. He did not know anything about engines, but he saw that it was quite shiny. He pretended to check out one part and another.

"How much rego left?"

"Another four months," said the mother, handing him a glass of cold water.

"I'll take it," said Hank. "I'll pay cash. Where can I find a swag?"

"I'll come with you," said the mother, handing him the key to the car. "You drive while I fill out the rego papers. Are you new in town?"

"Yes."

"For work?"

"I'm starting a business,"

"Wow, a business doing what?"

"It's a secret still."

"Oh, yes, of course, pardon my nosiness."

"It's okay," said Henk.

Even older women were handsome here. Independent and strong. He liked it.

"Give this man a good deal," she said to the swag maker. "He's bringing business to town. He has just bought my car."

"No worries," the swag maker smiled. "Single or double?"

"King," said Hank.

"Certainly. What colour would you like?"

"That brownish red," said Hank, pointing at a canvas roll.

"A thick mattress or a thin one?"

"Thick."

"It'll be ready at the end of the afternoon. It will be a big roll."

"Brilliant," said Hank. "Where can I drop you off, Ma'am?"

"I'll stay in the warehouse while you and Mabel deliver the goods to your shed."

Mabel, her name was Mabel. Yes, she is a real Mabel. I like Mabel. I might ask her out one day, he thought. Things were working out for him here. It was as if he were riding a wave. First meeting Blue at Chiffley's Resort, then observing the painting shed, renting a shed, Mabel's warehouse, the Cruiser, the swag....

It's meant to be, he thought. I've got more done today than in the past year.

At five in the afternoon, he had everything to start his painting shed. He rolled out the new swag, set his telephone alarm and stretched out on the red canvas.

I am not allowed to sleep here, Blue, but you can't prevent me from *falling* asleep here, he thought. "The devil is in the details, you greedy bastard," he murmured, and smiled.

*

Bettina was talking to her cocaine dealer. They were in the Homebush Bay apartment. This was unusual; normally, they met in a public place, a coffee shop or a gallery. But Bettina did not have to hide the dealer from Hank any longer because Hank was in Alice Springs for the second time and probably for good. The fool!

The dealer did not look like a dealer but rather like a university professor, with his fishbone jacket, narrow knitted tie, grey shirt and woollen slacks. He leaned forward in the leather Lay-Z-Boy and looked at Bettina compassionately as if he were a counsellor.

"You won't find anyone in Sydney to do that kind of job," he said. "We got to go somewhere else."

"Where," asked Bettina. It sounded like "Vhere".

"Nimbin in New South Wales," said the dealer.

"Nimbin? That hippy town near Byron Bay?"

"Yes."

"A hippy killer?"

"Hippies have evolved into desperate monsters," said the dealer with a little laugh. "They'll do anything for money. I know one who would do it for, let's say fifteen, twenty thousand."

"That's not much," said Bettina. "Will they do a good

job for that kind of money?"

"Yes. They are money hungry but also try to hold on to some values, so they sell their services cheaper than elsewhere. Drugs, fake marriages, prostitution, murder .... They have no idea what things normally cost. Ideal!"

"Hmm, I wonder what went wrong," said Bettina.

"In Nimbin everything went wrong," said the dealer. "Those guys don't carry phones; you must look for them in the wild, so to speak."

"How do I do that?"

"You would have to take me with you."

"And what would that cost?"

"Fifteen, twenty thousand, maybe more."

"Okay. Half upfront, half when the job is done," said Bettina.

"You watch too many movies. After I have introduced you is fine," said the dealer.

"Upfront is fine," said Bettina. I've got the money and I trust you."

The dealer stood up. "Thank you, Ma'am, shall we go then?"

"Go where?"

"To Nimbin."

"Now?"

"Yes. You will need to take the cash, whatever the killer needs from you, and a set of clean clothes. We'll be away for five days or more."

"Okay, give me ten minutes," said Bettina, leaving the room.

In her bedroom, she gathered some clothes in a small overnight bag. She took some of Hank's stuff from the bathroom and threw it in a plastic bag: a comb with his hair still on it, his shaving gear, his hand mirror, and some underwear.

"Which car do we take?" she asked when she returned to the living room.

"Yours," said the dealer.

"Okay. I need to go to the bank before we hit the road."

"No problem," said the dealer and slung his overcoat over his shoulder. He looked like a handsome Italian art dealer now. Bettina quite fancied him. It was pleasant to sit next to him in her dark blue BMW. He was the calmest person she knew. They did not speak much, but the silence between them was comfortable. They drove through the night, taking three-hour shifts behind the wheel. The BMW was silent and lay low on the road, smooth like a shark. German precision.

They slept at bland three-star hotels in separate rooms. Bettina booked herself an open one-way ticket to Germany.

They arrived in Nimbin on the third day at five-thirty in the morning and parked in the main street where a flock of rainbow lorikeets was eating from the rubbish strewn around. They stepped out of the car, stretched, and looked around.

"Ouch," said Bettina.

"Ouch," echoed the dealer. "How can they make it stink like this in a landscape like that?"

He gestured around them to the hilltops. It was getting light quickly. All the buildings were covered with flaking hippy murals and graffiti. Some chickens appeared from a grubby lane and joined the rainbow lorikeets. A barefoot woman walking two goats passed by, then a runner wearing a Walkman and nothing else. His limp member bobbed up and down. The dealer told Bettina they were waiting. They got back into the car.

"Lots of sitting going on here," said the dealer, pointing at the mouldy benches lined up along the pavement. "Christ, I hate this place."

After a while, a butter-coloured Merc rolled into the main street and parked about three hundred metres away from them. A couple of quiet seconds went by.

"Here it comes," said the dealer.

Suddenly, from all directions, from behind and underneath the buildings, like vermin from under a tile lifted from the grass, the junkies appeared. They crowded around the Merc and clawed at the tinted windows, screaming abuse at each other. A back window opened a little. Money went in; little plastic bags containing white powder came out and changed hands, while the screaming intensified.

It ceased as quickly as it had begun.

The junkies disappeared, the window closed, and the screaming echoed in the hills.

Now the dealer stepped out of Bettina's car and knocked on the driver's window of the Merc. He bent down to talk to whoever was hidden in there.

"Long time no see," came from the window.

"Do you know where The Werewolf is?" the dealer asked without replying to the greeting.

"Mick Eagerly? The Werewolf? He's around. He works part-time for the Veranda Café there, don't know his hours. But he's often in town. Just wait and watch. He does stand out nowadays, he's always bare-chested."

"Thanks, mate."

The window rolled shut and the Merc disappeared.

"Let's go," said the dealer to Bettina.

"Did you find what you were looking for?" asked Bettina.

"Sort of," said the dealer. "I park the car; you book two rooms at the hotel. One night will do for the moment." He pointed at a large building on a corner. "I'll see you on the front veranda on the first floor." He pointed upwards.

Bettina looked and nodded.

She was seated in a wicker rocking chair, with a cup of coffee on a rickety table, when he joined her.

"Perfect," he said, stretching in the other rocking

chair.

"What are we looking for?" asked Bettina.

"Leave it to me," said the dealer. "All we have to do is sit here and wait and watch. Worst-case scenario: It takes a couple of days. Why don't you get me a coffee?"

"Sure," she said and went downstairs.

They had breakfast and then lunch on the veranda, followed by beer, all dutifully fetched and paid for by Bettina. Then Bettina sniffed some coke to stay awake.

"You can go to bed, you know," the dealer said.

But she stayed and watched the main street with him. First, a lone street sweeper cleaned up what the birds had left.

"That guy has been doing that ever since I remember," said the dealer.

"Good on him," said Bettina.

"Filthy loser," said the dealer.

Around nine, the first hippies arrived at the scene.

"Amazing," said Bettina, "There are still so many of them. A whole village full."

"Yeah, old, ugly and disappointed," said the dealer bitterly.

At about ten, when a tour bus arrived, a group of heavily tattooed skinheads began to form in front of the lane they were facing. They hissed at the passers-by. Now and then, someone disappeared into the lane with one of them. Money changed hands, and God knows what else.

"They are the weed dealers," said the dealer.

"Jesus," said Bettina, 'it's all done in broad daylight. Are there no police here?"

The dealer pointed.

Bettina leaned over the balustrade. She could make out the blue police sign on a pole. "They are right in town," she said.

"And into it up to their eyeballs," said the dealer.

"Really?"

The dealer did not bother to answer. Instead, he pointed at a group of brick buildings beyond the lane they were facing. "You know what those buildings are?"

Bettina looked. "School buildings?"

"Right. Now look at these skinheads and tell me what you see."

Bettina observed the group for a while. They were intimidating in the way they took up a fair stretch of sidewalk, holding their arms a bit away from their sides, looking around like eagles, and making sharp turns of their heads.

"They are young," she said after a while.

"I was nine when I started there," said the dealer. "You cannot imagine how I fucking hate this place."

"So, straight from school into dealing," said Bettina.

"That's exactly right."

"Jesus," said Bettina.

"Say no more," said the dealer. "I never used the

stuff, knew instinctively not to do so, still don't. But that's because I got out, and that's not the case for these kids. They start doing chores for the older ones, fetch them coffee, lunch...by the time they're ten, they are smoking weed, and by the time they're twelve, they're on ice. Your killer is one of them. He's thirty-two and has two young children. Speaking of the devil..."

The dealer interrupted his monologue and ran down the wooden stairs. He stopped a bare-chested man in the street and talked with him for a while. They gestured and laughed. They walked to the hotel and disappeared under the veranda.

The dealer appeared alone at Bettina's side and said: "He will be sitting on the rear veranda, behind the café, with his back toward you when you enter. You can't miss him; he's not wearing a shirt."

"Yeah, I saw him."

Bettina slowly walked down the creaking stairs, crossed the wet floor of the still-deserted pub, and stepped onto the vast back veranda.

There was only one customer: his naked tanned torso shone as if it had been oiled. His long hair was tied in a ponytail and hung limply on his back.

"Yes, you can come over, I don't bite," came his voice.

Bettina walked around him and took the seat opposite him. She smelled him before she saw his face. A strong scent of coconut oil and sweat. Then she saw his face and was surprised by its friendliness. The eyes were incredibly blue, the sideburns very long, and they sat on his cheeks and chin like sunbeams on a child's drawing. She understood why they called him the Werewolf.

"Good morning," he said and smiled. His teeth were healthy and small, like those of a small mammal. "I know exactly what you want, so let's talk money."

"How do you...."

"Never mind. After we settle on the money, you give me all the details. I will do what I must and disappear forever from your life. If you don't pay me, I will kill you too."

"It's in Alice Springs," she said.

"Fifteen thousand," he said, 'Three upfront."

She hesitated.

"What are you afraid of?"

"No, no," and she realised she did not know her dealer's name.

"My dealer assures me you are good. I trust him."

"I am good," he said. "Also here," he pounded with his fist on his chest to indicate his heart. "And affordable. A rare combination, but there you are. It makes it possible for middle-class people like yourself to hire a..." his voice trailed away then came back strongly.

"When I am done, I'll text this number," He gave her a cheap mobile phone. "As soon as you receive the text, you destroy the phone and return to Nimbin. Leave the money in a shop named *Hemping High*, you can't miss it. Do not fly; drive. Do not even think about not coming back, I know where you live."

"Yes, okay" Bettina said and handed him a plastic bag. "All you need to know is in here, including some toiletries with fingerprints, hair, for DNA, etcetera. There's a pair of rubber gloves on top. There are three thousand dollars in the gloves. Please check it."

"I believe you."

"There's a photo of him in there, too. I do not know where he is staying, you will have to find him. As for the victim: the most successful art dealer in town. A woman. Linda van Halen."

"Okidoki," said the Werewolf.

He took the bag, peered into it briefly and walked away from her, through the pub into the main street buzzing with people. She saw tourists and skinheads, murals, hippies and chickens, but she did not see the Werewolf anywhere.

She went upstairs to the dealer and said: "It is done".

"Okay, he said, "let's get out of this hell hole then. We can be back in Sydney by tomorrow morning."

They bought some food in an insanely crowded shop that called itself a supermarket but in fact was a souvenir shop of sorts. It smelled of patchouli. They took three-hour shifts behind the wheel and were indeed back in Sydney the following day, without ever having spoken of what they had gone to Nimbin for.

Bettina bought some more coke from the dealer before they parted, sniffed it as soon as she was in the privacy of her apartment and went to bed with a stack of DVDs and books. She loved lounging in bed on coke. She ordered Chinese. She thought of the dealer. They had just spent nearly three days together. He had grown up in Nimbin. What a place; filthy and desperate. She shuddered. She did not even know his name. He did not know hers either, she realised. However, she could be wrong about that.

The Werewolf had said that he knew where she lived. Was her name on the mailbox downstairs? She did not remember. She dressed quickly, took the elevator down and looked at the mailbox. 'Hank Jefferson' it said. Fucking Hank! She took the lift back to her apartment and returned to the mailbox with a knife. She pried the name tag loose with the point of the knife and returned to bed, satisfied.

Fucking stupid deluded Hank!

*

Linda Van Halen opened the door to the back room of her gallery and placed the stack of mini paintings, a rare find, on a table, then smoothed her dress with two hands while wandering to the mirror on the wall. Humming to herself, she inspected her make-up: a thin layer of pale foundation, orange lipstick, and dark grey mascara. She sniffed; she wrinkled her nose. Was that oily coconut smell? Then, in the mirror, she saw something move behind her. She stopped humming and turned around on her heels. A blunt, heavy object slammed down onto her head, sinking into her skull. She heard the bone crack and fell forwards, her vision exploding into a million fragments and colours. She saw colours she had not seen before, causing her a wave of excitement...

She was dead before her body reached the arms that caught her. The arms put her into a large wooden crate, slammed a lid on it, and closed the hinge clips.

ART. HANDLE WITH CARE. THIS SIDE UP, read the label.

*

"I've left my wife," Hank explained to Caroline as if it had been his idea.

"I'm sorry to hear that," said Caroline, looking at her watch. "She's late."

"Who are we waiting for?"

"Linda. She was supposed to be here at seven."

"Are you really?"

"What?"

"Sorry I left my wife?"

"Eh, not really; you were miserable, and so was your lady, I imagine."

"True," he said. "A drink in the meantime?"

"Sure," she said, a little too eagerly.

"Red, as usual?"

She looked at him and winked. "Of course."

He studied the menu while she checked her watch. It was an old-fashioned silver one. "You must be the last person with a watch," he said.

"I know," she said, "I hate mobile phones. But now I want to borrow yours to give Linda a call."

He handed her his iPhone.

She dialled clumsily with her forefinger.

He laughed.

"No answer," she said. "How strange."

"Linda," she said to the voicemail, "It's half past seven. I'm waiting for you at Barra on Todd. Have you forgotten our appointment? I have a friend with me from

Sydney. His name is Hank. I'm using his phone. Call this number when you get this message."

"Something must have happened, a flat tyre or something," said Hank.

"Yeah," said Caroline vaguely, eagerly drinking the red wine.

"Let's order; then she'll turn up when the food arrives."

"We always have the mussels here."

"Mussels in Alice Springs? You cannot get a decent pair of knickers, but you can get a Belgian mussel pot?"

"That's why we come here. It's so exotic. Bras are more difficult, however."

"Huh?"

"You can't get a decent bra here either."

"Is that a dish? Bra?"

"In Alice Springs, silly."

"Oh."

"Where's bloody Linda? I'm getting worried."

"She forgot; perhaps she's turned her phone off..."

"We buy them online."

Hank looked at her, an eyebrow raised.

"Bras. We buy them online."

"Ah."

"Very unlike Linda. But let's make the most of it."
She raised her hand to order.

"Er, Hank," she said, slurping mussel soup from a

shell she had somehow attached to her fork. He studied the construction. The two middle prongs of the fork were on top of the shell, the two outer ones underneath, forming a slide-on spoon. He made one for himself just like it and began slurping the soup as she was doing.

"Yes, Caroline?"

"I'm not going to sleep with you this time."

"Ah, why not? Are you involved?"

"No. I want things to remain calm. Just me and my daughter."

"Sure," said Hank, feeling disappointed but proud he was not showing it.

"It has nothing to do with you. It's about me and my daughter, okay?"

"Okay."

"You might like Linda."

"I'm not here for sex, or a relationship."

"Then what are you here for?"

"I want to set up a business."

"What kind of business?"

"Aboriginal art."

"Well then, you'll like Linda for sure."

"Why's that?"

"She has the best gallery in town."

"Really, which one is that?"

"Fafaf."

"I've been there."

"Oh, so you know Linda already."

"Yes, she showed me around."

"Well?"

"Well, what?"

"Did you like her?"

"No, not like that. I like you."

"Well, thanks."

"You're welcome." He caressed her leg with his foot, but she did not respond.

"Let me try to call her again."

They got drunk slowly while Linda failed to show up and they talked about Alice and art.

*

The next morning Hank parked his Cruiser just around the corner from Blue's shed in a position that Blue could not see from his roller door. Hank realised that Blue would not recognise the Cruiser either, so hopefully, it would take a while before he would realise what Hank was planning. And Hank only needed a while to establish his plan. He was wondering how Blue worked. Did he swap the Aboriginal painters around, women and men, per day, week, or randomly? He would soon find out.

The Aboriginal people began to arrive, on foot or in beaten-up Holdens and muddy Troopies. He heard them screaming and carrying on behind Blue's shed, then Blue's booming voice:

"Only women."

He then heard the old cars start, and the people on foot came around the corner in a wave of laughter and shouting.

Hank stepped out of the Cruiser and waved at the men. The cars came around the corner too and Hank flagged them down in a patronising manner.

"What's up, Bro, your car broke?" a thin tall man asked.

"Need help?" another enquired in a soft shy voice.

"You mob want to paint?" Hank asked.

"Yeah Bro, you got a shed?"

"Follow me," Hank said.

The thin tall man beckoned to the others and said something in his rapid language.

Hank's heart was pumping hard. It is working, he thought, while getting into the cruiser quickly. He drove to the back of his shed with a flock of cars and pedestrians in his wake.

Hank gestured where to park the cars, well out of Blue's sight, in case Blue decided to take a little walk. He opened the roller door. His shed was set up in much the same way as Blue's, so the men stepped inside unsurprised.

On the floor were squares and rectangles of linen that had been neatly gesso-ed black, brown, or white. The stretch marks of the frames were visible. Along the walls stood ten-litre plastic buckets of paint, galvanised buckets with brushes and sticks and piles of mixing bowls, and carton board boxed with coloured chalk. A mountain of old rags was piled in the middle of the room, like a bleak Christmas tree.

Thirty-one men flocked into the shed and stood around in silent anticipation. Hank did not know what to say to break the silence.

"You got coffee, Bro?" the thin man finally asked.

"Not yet," said Hank. "I'll get it once you're all painting. Can everyone here paint?"

"Of course," said the man quickly and said something in his language. A couple of men laughed and said something in another language, whereupon others laughed and said something in yet another language. This went on for a while. How many languages are spoken here?" asked Hank.

"Many," said the man.

"How many?" asked Hank.

The man looked at him puzzled, then began counting on his fingers: "Warlpiri, Anmatjerre, Pintupi, English, Luritja, Arrernte, Pitjantjatjara, Ngatatjara..."

"Far out," said Hank. "How many do you speak?"

The man looked at his dirty fingers. His fingernails were long and black. "Five," he said after studying his fingers for a while.

"Well done," said Hank. "I only speak two."

The man looked at him in surprise. "Two? Which one?"

"English and German."

"What's German?" the man asked.

"The language of Germany in Europe," said Hank. "Where are you from?"

"Most of us mob is from Yuendumu," he pointed at the men around him while he summed up: "Wanu, Yajalu, Yuwarli, Hazel Creek, Jilla, Julpugu, Jungarayi, Mt Denison, Wayililinypa,, Yaripilangu, Yumurra...."

"I've never even heard of these places," said Hank. "Where are they?"

The man took a dotting stick from a bucket and walked to a dirt patch outside. He knelt, smoothing the dry dust with his hand and began to draw a map.

"This: Tanami Desert, this: Western Desert, this: Simpson's Desert," he said, expertly dividing the land he had drawn. Then, using the point of his stick, he marked the places: "Yuendumu, Wanu, Yajalu..."

The others crowded around him and noisily added places, pointing their fingers to the ground: "Yuwarli, Hazel Creek, Jilla, Julpugu, Mt Denison, Wayililinypa, Jungarayi, Yaripilangu, Yumurra.....".

Hank whistled. "You've gotta take me there one day," he said.

The man laughed softly. "Nothing there," he said.

Hank took the stick from the man's hand and drew a rough map of the world. "Australia, America, Africa, South America, Europe," he said, driving the stick's point into the sand: "Germany."

Hank now extended his hand. "I'm Hank," he said.

The man did not look at him while he returned the handshake awkwardly. Hank turned to the men inside and said loudly: "I am Hank."

They did not react. They just stood there. Silent.

"Let's start the painting," said Hank.

"We're hungry, Bro," said the thin man.

"I still have to go to the shops," said Hank.

"First tucker, then paint," the man said.

"Okay," said Hank, "you come with me; they wait here."

"What's your name?" Hank asked when they were seated in the Cruiser.

"George," said the man.

"Okay George, which supermarket?"

"Coles," said George.

Two hours later, Hank and George unloaded from the Troopy a fridge, a plastic trestle table, an electric kettle and twenty-seven Coles bags full of food and beverages.

The men were sitting patiently on the concrete floor.

George sat down and Hank put some food in the fridge and some on the tables.

"I need some help here," he said loudly and looked around the group. Nobody moved.

"Seems we need some rules here," he said and pointed: "You, boil the kettle. You, butter the bread. You, divide the chooks...."

Nobody moved.

Hank looked around and then put everything in the new fridge. "No help, no food," he said, looking at George for help.

"You got a shower Bro?" said George.

"No."

"We are dirty," said George. "We want a shower."

"Tough luck," said Hank.

"No shower, no painting," said George.

Hank put a hand in the pocket of his jeans and held up a roll of cash. "Will this help?" he asked.

There was a stirring and a mumbling. "How much for a painting?" George asked.

"That depends on the painting," said Hank. "You paint, I tell you what I want to pay for it. Pay time: five o'clock every day."

"You pay cash?" George asked, and he sounded somewhat excited, somewhat surprised.

"What? Do others pay into your bank accounts?"

George shook his head. "They pay in cars, tobacco,

wheelchair, computers, booze, taxis..." he was using his fingers again. "Sometimes cash too."

"Ah," said Hank. "Well, here, it's cash only."

"Food is free and shower is free," said George.

"Okay, okay, I will build a shower, but that will take time."

"We want a shower very soon."

"I will build a simple one today," said Hank. "You can take a shower this afternoon."

"Okay," said George.

"Shall we start, then?"

Nobody moved; all sat still, looking at the floor.

"What?" Hank roared. His voice echoed against the walls.

"Shower first," said George.

"Okay, okay," said Hank. "Wait here you lot."

When he came back with a drill, a couple of spanners, a jumbo pack of soap bars, four large hooks, plugs, a roll of thin rope, four camp showers, one long hose, a hose connector for the tap, four short hoses and a four-way hose connector, the men were still sitting patiently on the floor. They looked at Hank from the corners of their eyes while he drilled holes in the shed's outer walls next to the roller doors, screwed in the hooks, connected the hoses, filled the water bags and hung the black bags in the sun.

"Nobody inclined to help yet?" he shouted.

There seemed to be some negotiating going on in

several languages, and Hank grew hopeful.

"Only four showers," said George.

"Yes, what do you expect? Thirty-one showers?"

"Only four hot showers at the end of the day."

Hank dropped his spanner, placed his hands on his hip like a lady and sighed.

This made some of the men laugh softly.

"The water will be warm in an hour, so four take a shower each hour," he said. "Can we start to paint now?"

"First food and coffee," said George, pointing with his chin to the fridge.

"You win," said Hank and began to unpack the fridge onto the table again. He buttered the bread and boiled the kettle, set out the coffee, the milk and the sugar, divided the roast chickens in small portions, unwrapped the paper serviettes, cut the cucumber and the tomatoes, spread out the slices of cheese, arranged the knives and spoons in a cup like a bunch of flowers, lined up the salt and the pepper and the barbecue sauce and the tomato sauce, and bowed.

"Gentlemen," he said, "your breakfast is ready."

The men ate in silence; like monks, they seemed to take their food very seriously. They then sat on the floor with their canvasses and painted, while Hank installed security cameras in all corners of the shed. A monitor and computer went on his desk. He made sure the men knew what he was doing and why. They had better understand from the start that he favoured a zero- tolerance policy when it came to stealing.

*

Jay Gordon was wheeling his chair through the sand, leaving the community behind him. Immediately he was surrounded by horizons. The red desert was dotted with green because it had rained lately. It was hardly a path he was on and the going was tough. His hands and arms worked well and he breathed heavily through his teeth, between which he held a bunch of painting brushes. The leather of his seat creaked rhythmically. On two improvised wooden shelves, his limp bare feet turned inwards as if talking to each other, and his pelvis was like a rag doll's, so thin, but his torso was powerful as a weight lifter's. On his back hung a roll of linen and an old leather bag from which a water bottle protruded. Sweat poured over his face, shaded by an Akubra so old that it was sixty per cent holes.

Miraculously he managed to manoeuvre his wheelchair up a low hill until he reached a large flat rock. Everything was flat in this landscape, eroded by time to mere horizontals. Next to the rock was a thin gum tree, providing some shade.

He sat very still, panting. He spread his canvas over the rock, filled a cup with water from his bottle, lined up six jars of acrylic paint, put the brushes in the pink hollow of his hand, spat on them, and began to work.

He loved coming to the rock to paint. It was quiet and slightly cooler here than in the community, where one drunk idiot or another was always disturbing his work.

Tender and thoughtful, he used the brushes carefully to create an intricate pattern of vertical strokes that danced this way and that, like flames, close together. He never painted anything other than his beloved fire-dreaming. He started at one end of the canvas and rhythmically worked his way to the other side, never missing a stroke, humming to himself while he painted, a soft growling that came from deep inside his chest and that was for his ears only. He found comfort in his humming and in the mechanical movement of his hand, the shimmering of the reds and pinks and purples in the corner of one eye and the blank black of the gesso in the other.

He had covered about a third of the stretch of the canvas when he felt the need to drink. He stretched his back and drank deeply from the bottle. He did not swallow but spat the warm water over his hands. He closed his eyes and leaned back in his wheelchair, his chest rising and falling, his arms limp, his wet hands like small animals alive in his lap.

With a little bit of luck, he could finish this canvas today.

Blue would buy it for sure; Blue almost always bought his paintings. Maybe he could get a second-hand Holden for this one.

He opened one eye and peered over the endless plain before him.

He opened his other eye when he spotted a Troopy in the distance.

Who could that be at this time of the day? And not on the track too, but right smack in the middle of the plain. He could not hear the motor, but the Troopy came so close that he could see the figure behind the wheel. The figure wore the same kind of hat as he did, a Cattleman, and seemed unsure of where he was going. What idiot went off-track all by himself around noon? It was a white fella; that much was clear. He looked quite feral.

Jay sat as still as the rock beside him and watched as the Troopy came to a halt and the man jumped out of the driver's seat. He was wearing army camouflage pants and heavy boots and walked to the rear end of the Troopy, opened one of the back doors and took out a shovel with a long handle. Then he walked to the front of the Troopy again and looked around him, peering at the rock and the tree, but did not spot Jay in his wheelchair. He was ready for some sort of action, that much was clear.

The man began to dig. He dug like Jay wheeled his chair, tireless and without breaks, while Jay sat still as a lizard in the sun, watching. Sometimes the man drank from a flask that hung from his waist, and then he feverishly continued.

After what seemed to Jay about two hours the man had dug an enormous hole. Still the man took no break. He walked to the back of the Troopy, opened the second rear door and dragged a large wooden box to the sand below. It was one of these art crates that Blue used for storing and transporting pottery or large rolls of canvas. Jay could see the black lettering, although he could not read it. There were arrows on the box too.

The man was dragging the crate to the hole. The crate was heavy and the lone figure had to use all his weight and strength to get the crate to the rim of the hole. Once there, he slowly tipped the crate into the hole.

The shovel was at his side, leaning against the bumper of the Troopy, and without delay he began to cover the crate with sand. Again, he did not tire. The red sand piled up, and the remaining sand he threw in the tracks of the Troopy until there was no trace of the pile or the hole.

He stood there for a couple of seconds, hands on his hips, looking around him, then threw the shovel back in the Troopy, closed the doors and drove off into the direction he had come from, following his tracks.

Jay blinked. The whole scene had taken about three

hours.

Jay did not move but began to grin. In there must be some pretty expensive art. Otherwise, the guy would not have buried it. And he, Jay, knew where it was. He was the only one who knew where the man had buried the crate. Finally, finally, finally, he, Jay was lucky.

He sat next to his rock, breathing slowly and grinning. He could not continue painting, so he slowly rolled up his canvas. He screwed the tops on his jars of paint and headed down the hill, brushes between his teeth.

The sand was at its hottest. He knew from its fierce glow that it must be around three o'clock.

He had to find his friends before they were too drunk.

He dumped the painting and his painting materials on top of an old mattress in the garden of his Auntie Betty's overcrowded house and wheeled himself to a house opposite that was in an almost unbelievable state of disrepair. On the dusty patches of grass, amongst hundreds of dried dog turds, empty cans and old chicken bones, were Muddy, Gray, and Floyd on a low sofa that seemed to be held together by its filthy flowery fabric. They were drinking beer, not rum, which was a good sign. Jay told them quickly what he had seen, his grin wider than usual. His strong arms gestured broadly, indicating the size of the art crate. Soon they were all grinning widely, exposing teeth in various stages of decay, while walking to an old Ford Falcon station wagon with one wooden wheel.

They had to dodge Auntie Betty, who wanted to bash Jay on his head with a serrated branch of mulga for leaving his painting stuff out in the open, in her garden, on her mattress.

She screamed like a pig being skinned alive.

She swore like there was no tomorrow.

She went for all of them when she couldn't get to Jay. But Floyd, Gray and Muddy plucked Jay from his wheelchair and planted him in the passenger seat of the Falcon, fending off Auntie Betty as if she were an annoying fly.

With Floyd behind the wheel and Gray on the bare floor in the back, they did a couple of burnouts around the screaming woman and then raced out of the town into the desert, leaving a black trail of smoke behind them from the broken exhaust. Auntie Betty ceased screaming as abruptly as she had started and walked away from the stinking plume, mumbling to herself.

Jay watched them from the passenger seat. Their digging was frantic and uncoordinated. They used large sticks and their hands. Sweat was dripping everywhere as they groaned and swore and laughed loudly.

Jay giggled in an excitement he had never felt before. He, Jay, had struck luck. He had never felt successful in his whole wretched life. And it felt good, he was on top of the world, ah, it was wonderful.

The diggers' sticks hit the hard lid of the crate. It sounded pretty hollow, Jay noticed with a pang of fear. But nah, a bloke would not drive all this distance and dig like that to hide an empty crate.

The men used their hands to get the crate free. Large, strong beautiful black fellas' hands, thought Jay, for the first time in his life, proud of the mob he was from. He looked at his own hands, and they seemed to him the most beautiful intricate things in the world. His hands itched with a longing to help free the crate. He moved the fingers this way and that, clenched his fists, unclenched them....

When they had freed the crate from the gripping sand, they lifted it into the back of the Ford, and Gray sat on top of it, panting and soaking wet with sweat. "It's heavy, alright," he said.

They drove the Ford to town while discussing where they would open the crate.

"Auntie Rosie's place? She's in Alice Springs with her daughter."

They parked the Ford behind the Mission House where Rosie lived, the back pointing to the front door of her house, the broken exhaust pipe pumping black smoke and soot.

While Grey and Floyd carried the crate inside, Muddy went to get some power tools. It was pitch dark now. Gray pointed his torch at the crate: THIS SIDE UP it said. Large padlocks hung from all four clip locks. Floyd was already picking at one with a straightened hairpin and a knife that he carried in his pocket for occasions like this. Muddy worked on the other locks with an angle grinder.

Jay was sitting on a chair at the head of the crate, shouting encouraging words: "Yeah!"

"Get'm."

"Fuck!"

"Shit yeah!"

Finally, the lid sprang free, exposing a strip of the dark interior of the crate. They opened it to the light and peered inside, adjusted their eyes and the position of their heads as if to make sense of what they were seeing, and jumped back in horror.

In the crate was a dead white woman in a patterned dress showing prints of bottles. Orange high heels on her feet lay at an awkward angle. She was wearing a pair of glasses, the lenses broken. There was a massive hole in her skull. There was blood everywhere. Dried, stinking blood. Her brains were falling out of the hole in her head. In her hand was a tiny painting.

Gray vomited violently, the stream landing half in the crate, and half next to it on the concrete floor.

The stench of him made the others throw up too.

Jay bent forwards and slammed the lid shut. "We need to get it back in that fuckin' hole. Now." he said, his face ashen.

*

"Someone has been in my house," said Rosie. She was furious.

"Did you not lock your door again, Rosie?" the policeman asked.

"Nah," she said.

"Why not?"

"'Cause I never lock my door. They get in if the door locked too."

"Anything missing, Rosie?"

"Nah, just vomit all over the place and power tools and things."

"You are missing power tools?"

"Nah, they left them there."

"Let's go and have a look then. You came here by car?"

"No, on foot."

The policeman held the door of his Toyota open for her. "Let's go."

"No bloody night patrol," said Rosie, sitting in the passenger seat of the police car. "I used to be on night patrol. Now it's no good. We need the night patrol back."

"I know Rose, I know," sighed the tired policeman. "Now fasten your seat belt."

*

The *Alice Springs News* broke the news first on a Thursday, with a cover story:

TOP GALLERY OWNER IN ALICE MISSING

Then, on Friday, the *Centralian Advocate* followed with:

POLICE SEEK HELP IN DISAPPEARANCE OF
GALLERY OWNER

Both papers sported a photo of Linda Van Halen.

Caroline was in tears when she learned her friend was now officially missing. When the police questioned her, she realised how little she knew about Linda apart from her life in Alice Springs. She knew that Linda had an ex-husband somewhere in Australia, but she had no idea where; that Linda had two sons, somewhere in Europe – the Netherlands? Belgium? Ireland? She remembered the oldest was an architect, but she had no idea where or what his name was; that Linda's parents were still alive and divorced, somewhere in Europe; she was of no help at all. All she was able to give the police was Linda's telephone number and email address.

She pondered upon the question of how valuable friendships were in Alice Springs.

What motivated people, including herself, to move to this place on the event horizon of planet Earth? It was so close to the desert that death could be sensed and silence experienced. It was so far from what was generally seen as 'civilisation', yet it was so cultured in its representation of the culture of the oldest group of people still in existence.

Around it lay an ancient landscape, effectively cutting it off from anything significant but people. And these people, dressed in safari gear or Kmart clothes, interacted. Except Linda and a couple of other eccentrics, who bought their clothes elsewhere; abroad, online. They lived in the present and did not share much about what they had left behind in the cities, at the coast, or abroad.

Those from Alice sent their children to universities far away. And the children did not come back except perhaps to retire, so the town was full of the very young and the very old and the Indigenous and those who would rather not tell their story, because it was too sad, or too damaged, or too...

what had Linda's story been?

Caroline truly did not know.

*

Blue smiled when he read that Linda was missing. He was sitting behind his desk in his shed, his feet up on his desk. He immediately called Damport.

"Hey, have you seen the papers? Van Halen is missing in action..."

"Yeah," I've seen it.

"Sweet!"

"Yeah. Brilliant, isn't it."

Jay saw both papers on Monday, just after they had arrived in the community store. He bought both papers and raced his wheelchair through the dusty streets to find the others. Gray, Muddy and Floyd were sitting on their usual flowery sofa in the middle of a stretch of sand, gin on their breath, and fresh empty cans all around them on the ground in the dust.

Jay handed them the papers. Gray and Muddy couldn't read, so Floyd and Jay took turns to read the articles to them. English was not their first language. They read like children.

"That must be it," said Jay. "Now what?"

"What are we gonna do?" wailed Floyd.

"Nothing, man, nothing. They'll think we killed the kungka. No way we says nothing to nobody."

They all nodded. They all squeezed their lips together

as if to seal the deal. They were still sitting like that when a police officer walked towards them, Muddy's angle grinder in one hand, Gray's torch in the other, Muddy's extension cord hung over his right arm.

"Oh shit," said Muddy.

"Is this your gear, gentlemen?" the policeman asked.

"Yeah," said Muddy, "That's my angle grinder. And that's my extension cord."

"That's my torch," said Gray.

And why were these items in Rosie's house?

"We slept there," said Jay, "All of us mob. We were drinkin' and we slept."

"And you vomited too," said the policeman. "That's disgusting."

The four men looked at the sand.

"Now hurry up and go clean Rosie's floor, all of you. And while you're at it, clean all these cans up too, will ye?"

"Yes, sir," they said simultaneously.

"So what are you waiting for?"

"Now?" asked Muddy.

"Yes, now. When did you think? Next week?"

The three men jumped up from the sofa and slouched toward the Mission House, while Jay busied himself picking up the empty cans.

"A bit stupid, Jay, don't you think, to ruin an old lady's floor?" said the policeman.

"Yes, sir," said Jay while collecting the cans in his lap.

"We was drunk."

"What else is new?" asked the policeman.

"Nothing," said Jay. "I'm sorry."

"Bloody oath you're sorry," said the policeman. "Next time I'll put you blokes in jail."

"Yes, sir," said Jay.

The policeman walked away.

Jay sighed. He was trembling all over as he wheeled himself to a bin.

*

The two stacks of large paintings in Hank's shed were growing steadily. The left one was made up of paintings by women, the right one of paintings by men. The men's one was bigger.

Hank liked working with the men better than working with the women.

He felt sorry for the women. They often came with their small children. Hank also felt sorry for the children and could not resist cleaning their noses. And their ears. Oh, their ears! Sometimes cockroaches hid in them; all rolled up. He was afraid to damage their ears by removing the insects with tweezers. Many children were partially deaf.

The men, on the other hand, were proud. Real hard buggers, most of them. Hank knew how to handle them now. Most of the time, he tempted them with money to get what he wanted. Or with tobacco. Or cars. He had abandoned his cash-only policy in the first week he was interacting with them because it simply did not work.

The women would often paint just for food. He didn't like that either. It made him feel guilty and low.

He wasn't dependent on who was not painting for Blue anymore. The painters had brought other painters, and every day he found a group of them already waiting in front of the door of his shed, where he slept in his red swag, despite Blue's rules. He never saw Blue anyway.

He looked at the piles of paintings. It was time to start thinking about a gallery in town. He needed an assistant in the shed for the gesso- ing and the stretching. He reached for the Centralian Advocate and looked up the classifieds' numbers.

"Painter's studio worker wanted. $24 an hour. Casual, part-time."

He gave his phone number while looking through the paper. A front-page article caught his attention:

POLICE SEEK ASSISTANCE IN DISAPPEARANCE OF GALLERY OWNER

He read the article hastily. Good timing, he thought. Another reason to open a gallery soon, preferably in the main street.

Then he thought of Caroline. Linda Van Halen was Caroline's friend. Linda must have gone missing on the day he dined with Caroline. They had been waiting for her at the Chiffley resort. Should he call the police?

He grabbed his phone. He tapped his phone on his desk, thinking. He decided against it. Better to have nothing to do with it.

He called Bettina instead. "We have to sell the apartment," he said, without even asking how she was. "I want to open a gallery, and the timing is just right."

"Why is the timing just right?" she asked.

"The best gallery has closed. The owner is missing."

"Des einen Tod ist des anderen Brot."

"What does that mean?"

"You've forgotten your German already?"

"No, I just don't know what it means."

"One man's bread is another man's death."

"It's a she, a woman, and it's not certain she's dead."

"Whatever," said Bettina. "I agree about the apartment. I'll take care of the paperwork and email you the paperwork to sign."

"Thanks," said Hank. "I assume we go fifty-fifty."

"Sure," she said.

"I'll leave it up to you then."

"Okay, bye."

"Bye."

He could not believe his sense of relief when he hung up. She had not even asked how he was or when they would meet. He realised that he couldn't care less if he never saw her again. Everything seemed to be falling into place at last. That is what Alice Springs did to him. It was pretty brilliant. He decided to look for a place to start a gallery straight away. He had seen several empty shops in the CBD.

He peered into Van Halen's dark gallery, hands on the glass, his face in his hands. He could vaguely see the elegant curves of the spiral staircases, the tastefully modelled balustrade on the second floor. Pity he could not have this space. It was the best. Or could he? Who said he couldn't? He called Blue. "Blue, it's Hank. Long time no see." "Hank, how are you?"

"Doing all right. I have a question."

"Fire away."

"The gallery of the missing woman, is that rented, or does she own it?"

"Van Halen leases through LJ Hooker," said Blue. "Why?"

"I want it."

"Good luck."

"Thanks."

Hank turned his phone off and walked into LJ Hooker three minutes later. He felt good.

When he left the real estate office, he checked his messages. Some guy. Interested in the assistant position. Hank pushed the call-back button and got an answering machine. He left a message with the address of the shed.

"Come at ten AM tomorrow," it said.

At five to ten the next day the man arrived at Hank's shed. His Troopy was covered with red dirt as if it had been off-road for months. The only clean parts were two fan-shaped patches on the windscreen. Even the licence plates were covered.

"Holy shit, where have you been?" said Hank.

"Here, there and everywhere," said the man, "I've done more than four thousand K's lately."

"Traveling through?"

"Yeah." The man looked at Hank with piercing blue eyes. His enormous sideburns stood away from his face like sun rays in a child's drawing.

"I'd like to make some money for the next part of my trip."

"Where are you headed?"

"New South Wales."

"You want cash in hand?"

"Yeah, that would be good."

"Can you start today?"

"No prob."

"Where are you staying?"

The man pointed at his car. "In a swag on the roof. Can I park her here?"

"No problem. How long can you stay for?"

"As long as you need me, I'm in no hurry."

"I'll show you how it works; come in."

"Let me get my bag."

"Sure. You can put it in my office."

"Mind if I take my shirt off while I work?"

"No, that's okay, it can get hot inside."

An hour later, Hank's new worker was gesso-ing and stretching linnen while seven male painters emerged in whatever Dreaming they were working on.

Hank was filming them with his iPad. He was planning to show the film on a screen in the gallery. When he had visual footage of all painters, he interviewed each of them, recording what they told him. He was starting an archive of stories he would use for the text of the Certificates of Authenticity.

"What are you painting, Archie?"

"Ah, this Caterpillar Dreaming."

"Caterpillar Dreaming eh?"

"Yeah, famous story of my family. We travel far, you

know. Here and here and here." Archie pointed at several places on his map-like painting.

"Here," he pointed at an area that was very finely dotted in many layers, "the baby died".

His hands travelled over the oranges and reds. "And here we got the snake."

"How long did your family travel for, Archie?" asked Hank.

"Long time," said Archie.

"How long?"

"Looooooomg time," said Archie, puckering his lips.

"A year? Two years?"

Archie shrugged. "Don't know. Many days then, you know, sun, moon, sun, moon. Good days. Lots of water. Green time."

"Was it green in the desert?"

"Yes," Archie's hand was hovering over a green area in his painting. "We stay loooooong time. Every day. Kids were born."

"How old were you?" asked Hank.

"Just a kid. Big kid. Loooong time," said Archie and laughed.

"How many people, Archie? Were there many people then?"

"Oh yeah," said Archie enthusiastically. "Many more people. Kungka's look for food. Men sleep. Take bath. Many more come. Everybody Caterpillar Dreaming."

"So what is the name of this painting?"

"Tingari - Karrkurritinytja."

"What does that mean?"

"Name of that lake. Er, MacDonald Lake."

Hank was noting it all down on his notepad.

"Where were you born, Archie?"

"Lararra, east of Tjukurla in Western Australia. Then moved to Papunya."

"And why the MacDonald Lake?"

"I'm custodian. It's my Dreaming."

"What does that mean exactly?" asked Hank.

Archie looked at him and repeated: "I'm custodian. It's my Dreaming."

"So do you perform ceremonies there?"

Archie closed his lips and looked at Hank.

"What's the matter?" asked Hank. "You don't want to talk anymore?"

Archie just sat there.

"What?" Hank said loudly. "What's the matter all of a sudden? You're not going to tell me more?"

Archie showed no reaction.

"You want more money? Is that what you want? Are you going to tell me about your ceremony only when I give you money?"

Archie sat like a stone, his face blank.

Hank pulled a wad of money out of his back pocket and showed it to Archie. "How much to go to a ceremony with you?"

Archie looked at it and then began to move slowly. Hank looked at him in astonishment. It was like a film in slow motion. Archie stood up and turned around, so his back was to Hank and then sat down again. He remained that way no matter what Hank tried; with his back to Hank.

Hank gave up and drove into town for the paper. The headline now read:

GALLERY OWNER FOUND IN SHALLOW GRAVE 260 KM FROM ALICE SPRINGS

Hank read the article in his Troopy, the paper on his steering wheel.

Four Aboriginal men have led the police in Yuendumu to a shallow grave just outside Yuedumu in the Tanami Deserts. The grave contained the remains of Alice Springs gallery owner Linda Van Halen.

The Aboriginal men, whose identities have not yet been released, have been taken into custody for further questioning. The police are convinced they are dealing with a serious crime and do not rule out the involvement of one or more of the four men arrested. They are looking for further information.

Linda Van Halen disappeared without trace from her gallery on February 11 when she was supposed to meet a friend for dinner at Barra on Todd at the Chiffley resort. Van Halen did not show up and her gallery remained closed in the days after the dinner date. The police forcibly entered the abandoned gallery a week after Van Halen's disappearance. The gallery will be repossessed by the owners tomorrow.

If you have any information in connection with this case, please call Crime Stoppers 1800 333 000."

Hank hit the paper with his flat hand.

"Timing!"

He drove to the corner where the LJ Hooker offices were located. He was used to getting what he wanted, and he was after what he wanted. He would not take no for an answer; he had to have that space. Now.

When he returned to his shed, his new employee was engaged in a deep conversation with Archie. The two were sitting cross-legged opposite one another and did not look up when Hank entered.

"They've found the gallery owner," Hank said loudly.

"What gallery owner?" asked the employee.

"Never mind," said Hank. "Local news, I suppose. She's dead."

"Oh," said the employee and turned back to Archie. They were talking in low voices.

"What you're talking about?" asked Hank.

"Hey Hank," the employee said, "Archie here has

friends who want to come and paint."

"Are they painters?"

"One is, he usually sells to a guy named Blue. He always paints the fire Dreaming. His name is Jay Gordon."

"And the others?"

"They want to learn."

"How many of them?"

"Four, including Jay. They had a run-in with the law, they want to get out of the community for a bit, you know, start over in Alice Springs."

"What kind of run-in with the law?"

"The police just questioned them for a couple of days, that's all."

"Questioned about what?"

"They did not say."

"Van Halen, that's for sure. All right, they can come from tomorrow," said Hank.

"Well, if the police let them go they should be fine, no?"

His employee shrugged his shoulders: "I suppose."

Thus, Jay, Gray, Muddy and Floyd began to paint for Hank.

Hank was struggling with an enemy he had never encountered before; he was experiencing increasing feelings of guilt. It had started with Caroline. And then feeling guilty about Bettina. Damn Bettina, she had messed him up badly somehow. Bettina was well off; there was no reason he should feel guilty about her, after all, she was the one who could not have children, not he, but he felt it anyway; a nagging pull deep in his stomach, sharp flashes of emotional pain in his chest. What was even stranger was that he felt this guilt about Caroline too. It was as if he had violated a moral standard that he believed in; however, he could not even start to formulate what that moral standard was.

He wondered if he had somehow absorbed Bettina's moral standards. Bettina was full of moral standards. There were so many moral standards in Bettina that there was no room for anything else. Bettina lived by shoulds and should nots.

The feeling in his gut was even worse when he worked in the shed with a group of women and their children. It was as if their silent despair was somehow his fault. The food and money he gave them somehow never seemed enough.

The feeling kept him awake at night when he tried to figure out whether it was appropriate that he felt this way.

Had he hurt Bettina?

No. She did not know about Caroline. She might have guessed; that was all. She had joked about Linda van Haren. She had guessed it wrong.

Had he hurt Caroline? No. It was she who had told

him she needed time out.

Was he hurting the Aboriginal women and their children? No, he was making their lives better.

Or was he?

He loved it how, as soon as they stepped out of their chaos into the shed, they sat with their painting. Their shouting would cease abruptly, their pushing and shoving would stop, and they became quiet, focused, serene and dignified.

He provided them with shelter for the day, a shower, food and money. Still, the next time they arrived, they were dirty and tired, angry and noisy and most of the time drunk; the children often withdrawn.

Did he feel guilty because he was white?

Had the white man done this to them? It almost felt like a curse from God, but Hank did not believe in God and he pondered on this until the break of day. He did not feel guilty towards the black men who came to paint in the shed. He concluded that his guilt was arranged around one central theme: women and the children that they had or didn't have.

He dismissed the feeling of guilt as too mysterious and deep to deal with, too fr buried in his subconscious.

He had no time to embark on a journey of Freudian analysis. He had his hands full as it was. He trusted the feeling would sink back into his psyche if he gave it time.

But it didn't. It became a handicap.

Like a frozen shoulder.

Ah well, Hank thought, a frozen shoulder repairs itself too. It can take two years, but most frozen shoulders heal themselves. He could only hope it worked the same way with this guilt.

*

Jay and Archie taught Gray, Muddy and Floyd to paint. The three men were like a breath of fresh air in the shed as they had never painted before, and they loved it. They went at it like children, tongues between their lips, holding their breath, and then exhaling loudly in total concentration.

They used the brightest of colours: pinks, light blues, bright purples and yellows. A wealth of stories rolled from their lips.

Hank was filming it all and writing it down.

The employee, whose name he still did not know, could not prepare the canvasses quickly enough; such was their enthusiasm. And every stroke they put on linen was worth at least a dollar.

Only Jay was withdrawn and did not speak. Once he had helped set Gray, Muddy and Floyd to work, he sat in a corner as far away as possible from the new employee, whom he had recognised as the man who had hidden the crate with its unspeakable contents. He did not tell anyone but bore the terrifying burden of his knowledge alone.

He painted his Fire Dreaming slowly, stroke by stroke, flame by flame, as if to burn away the horrible memory. He did not understand how Gray, Muddy and Floyd could be so carried away, so delighted, and overwhelmed with the new painting experience, after what they had seen.

But they didn't know that it had been the new employee who had buried the crate. He alone knew that. He, Jay, had been the unlucky once again, as usual, as always. And he could not even talk about it with anybody. It made him mad, it made him sad, and it made him heavy with resentment. Resentment at the employee; resentment at this new white fella who ruled with money; resentment at his friends; and resentment at his whole life in general.

All he could do was paint. Stroke after stroke. Flame after flame. Every second a stroke.

He did not want to go to his rock anymore, as the spot reminded him of the unspeakable.

Jay did what he knew he shouldn't do; he began drinking, he began gambling, and within a week, he was sleeping in the dry bed of the Todd River, sniffing from a filthy plastic bottle, passing out in the sand under the bridge.

*

It did not take long for the police to come to Hank because many threads led to Hank.

It was Hank who had enquired after the Fafaf Gallery at LJ Hooker even before the body of its owner was found; Hank was the rising star in indigenous art in town now that Linda Van Halen had left the scene; Hank was the one who had been there with Caroline on the evening Linda Van Halen went missing, and the men who found the crate were now painting for Hank. It was pretty clear: Hank's name popped up a bit too often. The police decided to raid his shed.

On a bright Monday morning, they arrived unannounced. They had a search warrant and demanded that everyone leave the shed at once.

Red and white tape went around the shed. There were men in white disposable overalls, gloves and shoe covers everywhere, dusting surfaces for fingerprints with a nasty black powder, peering at things through magnifying glasses, using tweezers to put minuscule objects like hairs and even grains of sand into small plastic bags or containers, while Hank sat on his red swag in the driveway, swearing under his breath. They had confiscated his Troopy too.

Hank had sent his employee away as there was no

stretching and gesso-ing to be done, and the man had pissed off in his dust-covered Troopy in a hurry; the guy definitely did not like the police much. The police let him go without a glance.

Ironically, LJ Hooker called while Hank was sitting in his driveway, forlorn on his red swag, wondering what to do next, where to go....

He could take over the lease of the Fafaf Gallery. Would he come to the LJ Hooker office to sign it? Today perhaps?

Hank wandered listlessly over to the nearest white-overalled zombie.

"Can I go into town?" he asked.

"Yeah, sure, keep your phone on and leave your car here, we've got to do the car too. Don't leave town."

Hank sighed and called a taxi. "LJ Hooker," he said to the driver.

LJ Hooker's commercial property manager looked like a well-groomed poodle. A round dot of white hair on the top of her head, fluffy cuffs around her wrists. Her nails were polished a deep purple that seemed black as dog nails in the dead light of her office.

"Mister Jefferson," she exclaimed when he came in. "Can I offer you anything?"

"Breakfast, please," said Hank. "And a double shot of coffee."

She didn't miss a beat at this unusual request. A good

sign thought Hank - she was a shark. He liked sharks. He knew how to relate to them.

"What kind of breakfast would you like?"

"An omelette, smoked salmon, lettuce, mushrooms, no bread."

"No problem," she smiled and called reception.

"Now, Mister Jefferson, there is a problem we have to discuss."

"A difficulty." Hank paraphrased. He loved paraphrasing when presented with problems, it always worked. It kept you on top of the problem presenter.

"The police have searched the property, and the white walls, floors, stairs, the ceilings even, have been dusted with black fingerprint powder. It's tough to get rid of."

"Hard to remove..."

"We will, of course, compensate you if you would agree to...."

"I'll take care of it," said Hank, glad he would have something to do and a roof over his head in case the police took days or, God forbid, weeks, in his shed.

"I can recommend a good interior decorator if you wish..." said the poodle.

"I will do it myself," said Hank.

"In that case...."

Hank did not listen to the rest. He simply paraphrased.

"Two weeks' bond. Two weeks' rent in advance. GST not included. Condition report. Blah blah... ah, there is the food."

Hank signed the paperwork. His credit card disappeared and returned while he wolved the omelette down with the coffee.

The poodle dangled a bunch of keys from her dog-nailed finger. "I wish you all the luck in the world with your new business."

"Thanks," he said, absentmindedly wiping his mouth with a paper serviette and taking the keys from her.

There was a spring in his step as he walked to his new premises. The key worked smoothly; the door swung open without a sound. A strong smell of something chemical rolled over him, then the subtle smell of something sweet...

He stepped inside and walked around the rooms, his footsteps echoing in the emptiness. He estimated the damage: it would take him at least a week to get rid of the black powder and paint. By then, the police would probably have released his shed, and everything could return to normal. He did not think for a minute that the police would find anything that mattered in his shed.

That assumption was shattered the next day.

He received a phone call from the police: report to the police station at once to provide DNA samples and your fingerprints.

At the police station, he saw Blue and his Afghan friend,

apparently also waiting for DNA tests.

So he was not the only one being investigated. This cheered him up, but to his astonishment, a couple of hours later his DNA was found to match DNA on Linda Van Halen's body. And DNA from her body was found in his shed.

The police interrogated him for fourteen hours, but they had to let him go. He had an alibi for all his movements. He had been with Blue at the time of the murder. This did not mean he was off the hook, they explained, though they found it quite unusual that a suspect had a good explanation of all places he'd been to and witnesses to prove it. It looked as if he done it on purpose, to cover his tracks.

"Look," he said, "I get many people over in the shed daily. One of them could also have put the DNA there."

Hank had installed security cameras in his shed so that even his sleeping hours could be accounted for. The police confiscated the files from the camera's computer.

They were vague about where they had found the DNA.

Hank, to his outrage, was put on town arrest.

He decided not to think about it until he could do something about it.

Instead, he single-mindedly concentrated on the

removal of the fingerprint powder in the late Linda Van Halen's empty gallery.

He ensured he photographed the damage in case he could sue.

He made sure to wear a pair of waterproof gloves while he worked.

Where the fingerprint dust was on non-porous surfaces such as plastic, sealed ceramic or glass, he removed any loose substance by carefully brushing it off. He washed and wiped these areas down with warm, sudsy water. He put a squirt of dish-washing detergent into the sink and added warm water. He used a soft cloth to wash and wipe mirrors and lamps. He used Gumption for the walls and ceilings. He sprayed any heavily soiled spots, let it soak in for several minutes and used a clean cloth to blot them. He repeated this, if necessary, ten times, until the nasty stuff had gone. Then he rinsed the areas with cool water and blotted them dry.

Finally, the gallery was ready to be painted.

He carefully chose white paint and covered the whole gallery with three new coats, hoping the DNA problem would disappear in thin air.

He knew it could. When he was a manager, he had written all his problems of the day on separate pieces of paper in the morning and put them in his desk drawer. By the afternoon, more than half of the problems had disappeared into. Thus was the nature of problems, Hank knew they dissolved. This would certainly be the case with this insane DNA problem.

He worked without a break. Halfway through the work, his employee turned up to collect his wages. The man said he was tired of waiting around and was going back to New South Wales. Hank overpaid him so he wouldn't have to talk to him, and the man disappeared quickly when he realised how much cash Hank had given him in his open hand.

"Thanks, mate," he stammered and off he was, forever out of Hank's troubled hectic new life.

"Pfff," said Hank, wiping his brow with the back of his hand.

The gallery looked perfect. He mopped the floor and left.

When he unlocked his shed, he realised he would have to start all over again as everything there was covered with fingerprint powder too. Cleaning his car took him two days; carefully dusting the paintings took another day; the shed took a week.

He was now ready to hang some of the paintings and announce the opening of his gallery.

Blue was pissed off.

Damport and he had been called into the police station and were asked to provide DNA swaps. They had acquiesced; what else could they do? But it was humiliating all the same. And then there was Hank Jefferson, who had rolled into town loaded and was starting a gallery in Fafaf.

Just now that things seemed to be looking up, with Van Halen gone, another blow-in would open a bloody gallery. Jefferson meant business; Blue could sense that. So, he decided to ring the chick from Byron for some pleasant distraction.

"Hey you wanna go to my land for a couple of days? I need to get away."

"Can I bring a friend?" asked the woman from Byron Bay. "I've just met someone."

Male or female, Blue wanted to ask, but didn't.

"Sure," he said instead.

Stupid!

Blue was even more pissed off when he discovered the 'friend' was a daggy bearded bloke from the East Coast. His Troopy was so covered in dust that even the licence plates could not be deciphered. The car looked as if it was made of mud, except for two fan-shaped glass eyes where the screen wipers had worked their way through the red cake. The man had huge sideburns, which gave him a werewolf look.

"I need some fence wiring done, said Blue. "Easy, but it'll take quite a few hours."

"Sure," said the Werewolf.

Thus, the chick and the Werewolf followed his Troopy in their Troopy up the Merenee Loop. After they had checked out the small group of dongas, the fire pit and the gates in the fences, on his land, or rather his family's land, they lined up along the fence on his land and began clipping the wire in place while Blue cleared the grounds with his fork-lift.

An enormous pile of firewood was the result. Good dry old wood; a lot of kiji too, that stuff burned hot and long. From his high position, he could see the affair along the fence solidify; the flirting, the touching, the laughing.

Those two were having a good time along his fence. Shit! They worked effortlessly, clip after clip, towards the horizon, where the sun was setting.

"This is good fun," shouted the chick, "I could do this for the rest of my life." Furiously he changed to the tractor and dug some trenches while his guests entered the kissing stage, their faces hidden away from him by the bloke's Akubra.

What did the bloke have that he did not? The bloke was younger, the bloke was probably from around 'Byron' and engaged in some alternative healing practice.

By the time it got dark, and they started a fire, it was clear that the chick would share one of the metal beds around the fire with the Werewolf and not with Blue. Shit again!

Blue watched the starry night tumble around him while he listened to their lovemaking. The bed squeaked, the bloke groaned, and she, well, she faked it, obviously, with these little cries of hers.

He peered around for a scorpion or a snake to put in their bed, as a joke, but could not find one. Around midnight a herd of bull camels crossed their camp, producing the scariest sounds and leaving a track of dung.

The next morning, when Blue was collecting the dung, the chick announced she was hitching a ride to the east coast with the Werewolf.

Blue rekindled the fire and cooked a breakfast of baked beans and tea, while the Werewolf was texting on a cheap mobile phone. Blue then escorted the giggly couple back to the Merenee Loop and off they went down the Loop in the clay-caked Troopy.

Blue spat in the sand angrily as soon as they were out of sight. Could nothing go right for him these days?

Look at me! He thought. Slaving away on my family's land, alone, abandoned by everyone.

He had hoped his family would join him on the land he had put so much energy into getting. It had taken him years of land-claim paperwork. Getting the machinery there and the dongas, had left him broke. He had hoped his family would help him, that they would be reunited on this land.

But his mother preferred the casino, and all the others preferred to pass out in the dry riverbed in town. They did not give a damn that they had been born here on this land, somewhere under a tree in a creek. They were ashamed of it.

Blue had hoped that they would come and paint here. That's why he had built the shade house, just a roof on a central pole, no walls.

He had hoped that they would come and dry out here. Instead, they had beaten him up when they learned he would not provide the booze.

"We can make money together," he had argued. But they had only been interested in short-term desires.

What would he do here alone on a piece of desert bigger than England, where camels roamed wild, so he had to build expensive fences to keep them out?

Maybe he should start a camel farm? Or shoot the bastards and start a dog food factory?

He shook his head. He had no money, and the banks would not even look at him, even though he owned a piece of land bigger than England.

He stamped on the sand with his Santa Fe. What was the use of land when one could not mortgage it? The government wanted to look good; show the world that action was being taken in favour of their Indigenous population. Crown land was given away to those who could prove their families had lived there. Blue had taken a couple of officials here, and he had shown them the grinding stones of his grandparents. The stones were hidden in a clay pan under some shrub. He had described them in detail to the officials and shown them how they were used, feeling like an idiot, sitting in the sand grinding the top stone over the bottom stone, as if it was not obvious how a pair of sandstones worked. The officials had videotaped him.

The government wanted him to remain in the dirt like he had sat that day with the grinding stones. That was what all white folks wanted for the Aboriginal people. They wanted them near the earth, dancing and singing and painting their bodies and using grinding stones. And when they painted on canvas, they preferred earth colours. White man wanted Aboriginal man to go 'back to nature' so that white man did not have to do it. Thus, the Aboriginal man was fulfilling the romantic dream of the white man.

Again.

Damn!

Blue jumped in his Troopy, and drove back to his fire pit. In the glowing embers, he found the Werewolf's cheap telephone, all melted and bent and partly exploded. He chucked it back in the sand, extinguished the fire and raced down the Merenee Loop, back to Alice Springs.

He fishtailed dangerously.

Fuck the land!

Even the chick from Byron had preferred the hairy bloke from the East Coast, who did not own a brass razoo by the looks of it, over him, Blue, who owned a kingdom larger than England.

Blue pulled an ugly face and looked at himself in the mirror. "Byron!" he said sarcastically through the corner of his mouth. The white folks who cared about Aboriginal people were often worse than those who didn't care. The ones who cared thought he had a golden light shining from his ass. They kept thinking he could levitate no matter how rough he was in the mouth. Anyway…

It was back to the early morning painting hunt, the tedious haggling with David Damport, the shed and the stench of unwashed children. Maybe he could sell some stuff to Hank Jefferson for the opening of the new gallery.

*

The text message came: "It is done."

Bettina drove to Nimbin alone this time. Her dealer

had assured her it was safer that way. A bag with twelve thousand dollars rested on the back seat of the BMW. The interior smelled pleasantly of leather. The trip took much longer than it had the first time. With the dealer. Bettina decided to take it slow and spend the nights in expensive hotels along the way.

The newspapers, the Internet and Hank had confirmed it beyond doubt: Mick had done his job. The gallery owner was dead. It would only be a matter of time before Hank was arrested.

She left the highway at Murwillumbah. The road deteriorated immediately. There were potholes everywhere. To make things worse, it began to rain hard. She zigzagged the BMW through the thick rainforest at twenty kilometres an hour. The roadsides were soggy, and noxious weeds with purple, red or yellow flowers were strangling the trees.

She began to think about Mad Max and Wolf Creek. She worried about the BMW on this road that looked like Swiss cheese.

Finally, the village emerged from the early morning mist; the two rows of buildings with the fading psychedelic murals; sitting Buddhas with a third eye on the forehead; roaming indigenous men, naked and carrying spears; soap bubbles; mandalas; and rainbows, lots of rainbows, oh, and dolphins too....

"For Christ's sake," said Bettina under her breath as

she brought the car to a halt.

She watched the flock of rainbow lorikeets pecking at breadcrumbs thrown onto the pavement. A rooster and a couple of chickens were crossing the road. The man with a broom was sweeping the whole length of the main street, first the left side pavement, then the right side. The very early-morning dealing around the butter-coloured Mercedes must have died down.

Bettina recalled the scene, like a Hieronymus Bosch painting that had come alive for four minutes or so; the ferals surrounding the Merc. The Merc gliding out of town, the grisly group that surrounded it dissolving and the street becoming quiet once again.

She heard the sound of the broom on the pavement: pfffft pfffft.

The street still had a peaceful, vague quality about it.

Soon the madness would break loose, she knew, but now there was just the sound of the broom.

She looked around. A red party dress was on a wooden bench in front of the School of the Arts. It was draped so that it seemed that the wearer had just evaporated. What had happened there? Why was there a limp red dress on a bench in the street?

Bettina stepped out of her car and draped the dress over her forearm as she looked for a shop called *Hemping High*.

She found it at the end of a wooden veranda. It was

still closed.

She shivered in the morning mist and sat on a bench. She put the red dress beside her. At five to eight, she saw the Werewolf. He looked at her and then looked away.

She did not react.

He opened the door to a café, started a coffee machine and began to put tables and chairs out on the veranda.

Bettina moved to a table.

After a while, he brought her a coffee. She drank it gratefully. Their eyes did not meet and they did not speak.

She sat motionless until a woman arrived with a key to the door of *Hemping High*.

The woman must have been over thirty but was dressed like a child. Her shoes were pink and her rainbow dress bore many ribbons. Her hair contained even more ribbons. When she opened her mouth to talk, Bettina saw she was missing some teeth.

"Top of the morn," she screeched in the voice of an old woman.

"Morning," said the Werewolf cheerfully.

Bettina nodded.

The woman turned to her: "What brings you to town so early, love?"

"I...I was actually waiting for you..."

"For me?" The woman laughed. "Wow."

She had long, thin legs that looked as if they belonged to an old woman, just like her voice. She walked to her shop with giant strides.

"Well, come in then, love. Are you after some crack, then?"

"No," said Bettina when they were inside, "I am supposed to drop some money off here."

The woman's eyes lit up. "Ah, you must be the woman from Sydney. Bettina?"

Bettina nodded and placed the bag with the money on the counter.

"All right, let me count that for ye, love, it won't take long."

The woman counted the eighteen thousand dollars with great expertise. She repeated her rapid counting of the bills as if she was preparing a deck of cards to be shuffled.

"That's exactly correct, love," she said. "Is there anything else I can do for you today?"

Bettina looked around, at the wooden boxes in the shape of kookaburras, tea towels with hemp leaves on them, ceramic crocodile heads and garden gnomes. Claustrophobia overwhelmed her.

"No, thank you."

She walked quickly onto the veranda and sat on the bench again next to the dress. The Werewolf brought her another coffee. A scruffy old man walked by carrying a marijuana plant in a blue pot. He was limping. The plant had only grown a couple of young leaves.

Three police officers came from the other side, patrolling the empty street. The old man quickly parked the plant in the pot on the corner of the School of the Arts and walked on. However, he was seen by the three police officers. They ran after him. One police officer grabbed the plant in the pot, while another officer arrested the man, turning his arm behind his back. They marched off into the direction of the Police Station: the officer with the plant in the pot in front, then the officer with the old dude, then the empty-handed third officer. The officers were fully armed, Bettina noticed.

She stood up. She felt depressed. There was nothing she could do other than go back to Sydney, sell the apartment, fly to Germany and wait for Hank to be arrested. And then? Then what?

On her way to the car, she picked up the red dress and put it into her bag. She did not know why. Perhaps she needed a trophy.

When she drove past the café, she saw the child-woman hand the bag with money to the Werewolf, out in the open, in broad daylight.

She checked for cameras and saw them pointing at the street. She did not see any cameras pointing onto the veranda. Relieved, she started the CD player.

When the village was well behind her, she sent a text message on the cheap mobile the Werewolf had given her.

"It is complete."

Then she called Crime Stoppers and indicated that Hank had been the killer. When she was done, she tossed the device through the window into the thick vegetation at the side of the road. All that now remained to remind her that she had hired a killer who had killed a woman she did not know was a dirty red dress.

*

Jay wheeled himself in his chair through a narrow lane towards the Mall, a small, clumsily painted canvas on his lap. His hair was matted with dust, his feet bare, his eyes glazed. He felt as if he had a fever.

In the lane was a café with a busy al-fresco area.

Jay stopped at every table and held his painting up to whoever was eating and drinking there. The tables were covered with colourful juices and fragrant coffees, high stacks of sandwiches dripping with egg yolk. Jay's mouth was watering, but he had no access to any of the abundance displayed. He begged for a piece of toast but met only stony faces, and he moved on to the next table.

"Hey, I'm hungry, man."

He held up his painting, offering it for a piece of food. No one looked at it. He seemed invisible, as was his painting.

He felt dehumanised.

He patted the painting as if it needed encouragement and wheeled himself into the Mall, where he could hear the sound of a didgeridoo, voices and the clinking of glasses.

Bright lights shone inside a building. He drifted towards it. A sense of homecoming enveloped him.

There in front of him, in the building, which was blazing with lights, were his paintings. They were stretched onto large frames. Spotlights lit them from all directions. They seemed to dance like fire against the white walls.

People wandered in and out of the building, holding drinks and eating exotic-looking snacks from tiny paper plates.

Jay asked some of them for food, but they ignored him.

He saw a big black-and-white portrait of himself in the window. His name was printed underneath it in large colourful letters. JAY GORDON. Above it, it said: FIRE DREAMING.

He pointed at the photo and then at his face.

He did not realise how good he looked in the photo and how bad he looked now. They did not recognise him. He wandered amongst them as if he were a ghost, the pitiful painting in his lap.

He wheeled himself into the gallery and read the

cards next to his paintings.

Fire Dreaming, Jay Gordon, 2013, $16,000; Fire Dreaming, Jay Gordon, 2013, $21,000; Fire Dreaming, Jay Gordon, 2013, $34,000....

How could this be?

He saw Hank's excited face towering above the crowd and headed towards him, the bodies only parting when he nudged them with the wheels of his chair. Finally, he reached Hank, who stopped talking and looked down at the tragic figure in the dirty wheelchair.

"Jay? Where the hell have you been?"

Jay opened his mouth, but he was speechless with exhaustion and hunger. He lifted his hand and pointed at the paintings around him, then at himself. Then it was as if he was disengaged from his own body; he seemed to be hanging from the ceiling. He saw his hand fall into his lap on top of the painting. Then he fell from his wheelchair onto the floor like a rag doll. The crowd widened its circle around him. A collective "Ooooh" seemed to blend with the sounds of the didgeridoo that came from the speakers next to where he hung suspended from the ceiling. He was vaguely aware of a sharp pain in his left arm.

He remained in this vague, split state of existence for days. His hearing sharpened, and his sight cleared.

He followed with mild interest what was happening to the dusty heap of a man that was him. First, he heard the ambulance's sirens approaching and saw how he was hooked up to equipment in the hospital. All that time, there was a quietness in him and a knowing. A calming knowledge that everything would be good from now on; he could take care of his whole family and friends. Because his paintings fetched enormous sums, and he was now rich and famous. There was an enormous photo of him in the Mall. All he needed was a good rest.

Hank's arrival brought him out of this state. Flopping back into his body felt like getting into a cold, wet diving suit.

Hank was shaking his shoulder.

"Jay!"

The lightness in his body was instantly gone, and his legs regained their usual heaviness. He struggled to move his lips. His tongue was dry and seemed too large for his mouth.

Hank was holding a drink. He cupped Jay's head in one hand and let him drink from a straw with the other.

"Hank," Jay finally managed to say.

"Jay," said Hank, "how are you feeling."

"Good."

"You don't look too good, buddy. Where have you been all this time?"

"The river."

"The river," said Hank and sighed. "You have been sniffing petrol."

Jay nodded: "But I'm rich now, boss."

"Rich? Are you? How did that come about?"

"I saw the prices."

"The prices?"

"Of my paintings."

"But Jay, I have already paid you for those, remember?"

Jay wrinkled his forehead. "When?"

"I pay you guys at the end of every day, remember?"

"But my paintings, on the white walls...."

"Yes, your paintings are in the gallery."

"And my photo..."

"Yes, your photo is in the window."

"I saw the prices. Sixteen thousand, thirty thousand..."
Jay giggled happily.

"But that money is not for you, Jay."

Jay's eyes grew big with surprise. "Why not?"

"I have to pay for the gallery, the electricity, the opening party, a sales employee..."

"You pay with my paintings?"

"With the money I get from your paintings and the paintings of others."

Jay thought about this. "Then the gallery is mine," he said. "And the others'."

Hank laughed in disbelief. "That's not how it works, pal. The gallery is mine."

Now it was Jay who laughed in disbelief. "How do you mean?"

"Because..." Hank shrugged his shoulders, and his

hands moved up.

Jay's equipment beeped.

"You are exciting the patient," said a nurse. "His blood pressure has just gone up. You must leave now, Sir."

Both men felt heavy; Hank with guilt and Jay with dread.

The next day a guard was placed by the door and Jay Gordon was arrested on suspicion of the murder of Linda Van Halen.

All evidence pointed to Jay. It was Jay who had led Gray, Muddy and Floyd to the body in the shallow grave in the desert. It was Jay who had encouraged them to put it back. It was Jay who had lied to the policeman about their presence in Rosie's house.

"He is very confused," said the Warlpiri interpreter to the Aboriginal Legal Aid lawyer. "He keeps talking about eh.. a werewolf."

"We should concentrate on his handicap," replied the lawyer. "How on earth can a disabled man bury a large crate like that?"

The interpreter put this question to Jay, who showed her his strong arms as if he were a body builder.

"Tell him being proud of his muscles is not going to help him in court," said the lawyer. "On the contrary."

Jay smiled. "I'm rich, I own the gallery," he said in Warlpiri.

The lawyer sighed: "Ask him if he can drive."

"He says the Werewolf did the driving, and then Grey, Muddy and Floyd."

"Tell him he is incriminating himself with that werewolf nonsense."

"He says he owns the gallery, and that his paintings are paying for it."

"Tell him not to talk about werewolves in court, for Christ's sake," said the lawyer, thereby cutting off Jay's only chance of redemption.

*

Hank sold all Jay's paintings that week. He was already planning the next exhibition.

Bettina had flown to Germany. Hank discovered she had taken a large sum of money out of their bank account. He let it slide. He would soon get half of the sale of the Homebush Bay apartment anyway. He hoped she'd never come back.

Bettina stepped into the arms of her waiting parents at Berlin airport.

"You are wearing a red dress, how unusual," said her mother.

Bettina did a stiff pirouette. The red dress bloomed. "Do you like it?"

"Yes, I do," said her mother.

Sharon and the Werewolf were taking it slow in the Troopy back to Byron Bay. Sharon had invited him to her house in "Byron" which he had immediately accepted. He had a bag of cash. They planned to set up a healing centre. Now that they had had genuine experiences with Aboriginal people and had soaked up their spirituality, they felt entitled to do this. They had been given a skin name and had camped on Aboriginal land, invited by an Aboriginal man, after all. They exchanged thoughts on how spiritual Blue was.

"Blue is not his real name, you know," said Sharon.

"Yeah, I thought so," said the Werewolf.

Blue was driving through the town of Alice Springs in the early morning, looking for drunks with paintings. It was getting increasingly difficult to rum panting sheds. The laws were changing. Art centres were taking over. Galleries had stickers on the door declaring they only bought from art centres. But Blue knew the painting sheds would always be there. They just had to go a bit further out of town. Maybe all the way to his land… Or he would start his own art centre. He was Aboriginal, after all… He could keep selling that way... He was careful not to share this thought with Hank. Hank would not last. Hank would make his money and piss off to where he came from…

Jay was waiting to be trialled and sentenced.

The police had questioned him so often and put so many suggestion in his mind that he did not know anymore what was reality and what was fiction. In the end, he had just said "yes" to every question, because that seemed to be what the police wanted. to hear They had given him blankets and hot drinks in return and his friends were allowed to be with him when he was questioned. This had had made him feel celebrated. He had never experienced so much attention. It felt good.

The lawyer had said that a combination of the laws of complicity and mandatory sentencing would cause him to be in prison for twenty years with no parole.

Jay did not care much. He had stopped trying to figure out how the white man's world worked.

Prison was nice, he had said to the lawyer. Prison meant three meals a day and a bed. What more did he need? He may even be allowed to paint. He had many family members who were in Alice Springs Correctional Centre on a regular basis. He had been there many times to visit. There was a special bus for family members' visits. Volunteers drove it.

"Don't say that to the judge," the young lawyer warned.

"Why not?" Jay had asked.

"Because it won't help your case."

"What's wrong with prison?"

"There is no aircon in Alice Springs prison, didn't you know?"

Jay did not bother to reply that he'd never had air conditioning. He did not even like it. It gave him the shivers.

Why did white fellas want to help Aboriginal people all the time?

This young lawyer, the bus driver, Hank..?

Did they not have problems of their own to take care of?

Why did Aboriginal people always have to change their ways?

They weren't doing anything wrong.

Why change, then?

Why were the white Toyotas of the white helpers everywhere, bringing change?

Jay hated change.

In his community, they called white fellas "white Toyotas".

Jay smiled. White Toyotas! Funny as hell!

"What are you smiling at?" asked his cellmate.

"White Toyotas," said Jay.

His cellmate understood immediately why this was funny. He smiled too. "How long are you in for?"

Jay shrugged. "On remand."

"Like the rest of us," said his cellmate.

"Then…. Loooong time," said Jay.

His cellmate stared at the concrete floor. "White Toyotas!"

Jay spread his powerful arms.

"Looooong time."

*

In the tangled wilderness next to a deserted road full of potholes in New South Wales, a damaged mobile phone sent a text to another damaged mobile phone buried in a fire pit deep in the red heart of Australia.

"It is done."

"It is done."

"It is done."

"It is done."

"It is done."

"It is done."

"It is done."

Lightning Source UK Ltd.
Milton Keynes UK
UKHW020653020223
416362UK00014B/769

9 780645 707403